The Map

About the translator:

Kate Webster is a translator of Polish to English based in London. *The Map* is her first book-length solo translation. In September 2018, she was selected for the prestigious NCW Emerging Translator Mentorship Programme and awarded a 6-month mentoring placement with renowned literary translator Antonia Lloyd-Jones. During the mentorship, Antonia and Kate co-translated a graphic novel, *I Nina* (by Daniel Chmielewski), due to be published by Uncivilized Books. Kate's translation of Marta Kisiel's story *For Life* was published in July 2020 by Vintage Books as part of an anthology, *The Big Book of Modern Fantasy*. Other examples of her work, including translations of essays and short stories, can be found on the websites of Przekrój, Eurozine and Switch on Paper. Kate is a member of the Society of Authors and the Translators Association, and now mentors colleagues as part of the ITI Polish Network mentoring scheme.

Barbara Sadurska **The Map**

Translated by Kate Webster

TERRA LIBRORUM

London 2022

Terra Librorum
London

First published as *Mapa* by Wydawnictwo Nisza, Warszawa in 2019
Copyright © Barbara Sadurska, 2019
Translation copyright © Kate Webster, 2021

Edited and proofread by Linden Lawson, Sean Gasper Bye,
 Eleanor Updegraff
Cover design by Mimi Wasilewska
Typeset by Mimi Wasilewska

ISBN 978-1-914987-00-7
ISBN 978-1-914987-02-1 (ebook)

Printed in Poland

All rights reserved.

No part of this book may be reproduced, stored in a retrieval system, or transmitted in any form or by any means, electronic, mechanical, photocopying, recording, or otherwise, without the prior written permission of the Publisher.

www.terralibrorum.co.uk

Contents

Insomnia 7

The Map 35

The Butcher's Son 60

Faust 84

The Tomb 120

The Hospital 155

The Station 178

Insomnia

I shouldn't have agreed, really, but now here I was in the car, driving down this street I knew all too well. The same trees, the same tenement houses, the same people. Earning money, spending money, thinking about—

But this is Poland, money's not something we—

'We need to talk,' she said.

'Can I take you to dinner?' I said, and she agreed.

'We can eat together, just—'

I picked the restaurant.

So we drove down the street that we—

The car purred underfoot. Red at the crossroads. She leaned forward to turn on the radio. I saw her profile in the light of the street lamp. She adjusted her hair, uncovered her left ear. I couldn't take my eyes off it. A pink petal against a background as black as night. The driver behind tooted his horn. I pulled away a bit too abruptly, she looked at me. In disapproval?

I adjusted the rear-view mirror.

The voice on the radio announced that the station's Top Hits List in 1982 included the song 'I Can't Give You Much' by the rock band Perfect.

'Can I take you to dinner?' I said, and she said yes.

We had nothing. Her in her only dress. Charcoal-grey, almost black. I was working a few hours a week as a research assistant at the university. We ate carrots for dinner, and then—

'Your ear is like a snowflake,' I said, but she said nothing, just breathed.

And she looked at me with serious eyes that were not yet disapproving and said, 'Whatever you want, darling.'

'I picked that same restaurant,' I said.

'Whatever you want.'

Snow began to fall on the windscreen. I turned on the wipers, the bus in front slowed down.

Advertise with us.

'Change the station,' I said.

'No, no, why? Leave it on.'

I remember. Summer was over and we were staying in junior staff accommodation. She moved in with a box of books and a radio. Her father was having none of it. 'Stay away from her,' he warned me, before forbidding me from setting foot in his home in a residential neighbourhood where only surgeons and attorneys lived. And secretaries. Secretaries of state.

That house reminded me of Adrian Leverkühn's family home. Located in a quiet spot away from the centre, on a muddy street, near a wooden church. A mansard roof and five windows across the façade. I was reading *Doctor Faustus* at the time. Faust. How could I not make the connection?

Through the window I could see her father opening the drinks cabinet and pouring a glass of Johnnie Walker imported from Czechoslovakia. I knew that taste. I licked my lips. I felt a snowflake melt on my tongue. I was standing on the pavement. So there was a pavement, after all; it must have been laid by the Kraków townspeople, 500 years after Copernicus. I stood and looked at the brightly lit room as he entered, carefully closing the door behind him. Her father, not Copernicus. How many times had I been in there? I knew where the reviews were, and the annuals, where he kept the unread quarterlies and glossy magazines. I remembered the patterns on the rug and its left-hand corner, creased from the chair being pulled up to the desk. I even remembered the subtle movement of his right foot as he tried ineptly to even out the crease.

He sat at the desk and turned on the lamp—the lampshade had a pattern of purple and orange orchids based on Stanisław Wyspiański's design from 1899. Identical polychrome elements can be found in the Franciscan church where, a year later—

'Will you have dinner with me?' I said.

Yes. You said yes. Where, a year later, you said yes.

'What are we going to eat, darling?'

We had no ration coupons for meat or sugar. I'd scrounged cigarettes from a mate at the council. He always had cigarettes.

'Eating isn't important,' I whispered.

I swept back her black hair. Her ear like a petal. Like orchid petals.

Her father, bent over in the light of the orchid petals. I watched him open a drawer and take out paper and pen. A heavy fountain pen with a green barrel and arrowhead nib. I was standing on the pavement outside his house. I stood and looked through the window as he removed the lid from his heavy, gold-nibbed pen with his thick fingers. I couldn't see the details. I remembered. I remembered everything.

It started to snow, I was only wearing a suit jacket, I didn't even own an overcoat.

'What are we going to eat?' you asked, as I looked down at the menu.

'The duck is very good,' said the waiter.

I smiled.

'You eat meat?' Her tone made me want to deny it.

'No,' I stammered, embarrassed. 'But I do smoke. You want one?'

We used to smoke on the balcony in those days. You'd shiver from the cold.

'I don't smoke. Not any more.' She looked at the menu.

The waiter stood over us, showing no signs of impatience.

'Would you like to order wine?'

'I'm driving, but will you have something?'

I saw his every move: taking a sip of amber liquid from a tumbler of thickly cut glass, wiping the nib, and the sweeping handwriting of a self-righteous man who brooked no opposition, and anyway, who could have opposed him—after all, I was standing on the pavement, the pavement laid 500 years after Copernicus, on a winding street near the cathedral, beyond the light of the art nouveau lamp, and my feet were freezing—as he signed his name.

'We need money,' you said in a whisper, so as not to wake the baby. 'And you're on a research assistant's pay. We don't even have enough for a flat.'

Martial law had ended. Everyone was leaving.

'I can go to the US,' I said as we stood on the balcony. And you shivered and—

'Yes,' you said, 'yes,' dragging on your cigarette. 'Yes, go to the US. When you get back, we'll buy a Fiat and go on a trip. To Yugoslavia.'

'I'm driving, but…' I gestured towards her.

'I'll have the vegan tofu salad. And a dry white. Chiaroscuro.'

We ate in silence.

'You wanted to talk?'

She put down her fork.

'Yes. My father's made a will. And the thing is…'—a wisp of hair tucked behind her ear—'officially, you're still my husband.'

'Then the divorce will cost you half the inheritance.'

She looked at me suddenly with darkened eyes, her earlobe illuminated by the glow of the lamp. Art nouveau outlines. Pink snow in the black of night.

So he had written a script for us. He had signed the pact in his own hand.

The Alfa Romeo handled surprisingly nimbly. It followed the road well, reacted quickly to the accelerator. I found pleasure in the bright, leather interior, in holding the leather steering wheel and the gear stick adorned with the same, slightly shiny, soft leather. I much prefer European cars with manual gearboxes. In the US I go for automatics.

On the way back, I changed the radio station. I glanced in the rear-view mirror and, stroking the leather steering wheel, drove towards the city.

Night fell, invisible from beneath the street lamps and illuminated windows. I went back to the hotel. I didn't unpack my suitcase. The next day I was meeting my daughter, whom I hadn't seen since leaving for the US. Not counting the photos sent to me every Christmas.

It was snowing. I looked out into the street. The Alfa Romeo was waiting patiently under a soft layer of powdery snow. The scene sparked a fantasy, a desire to drive somewhere far away. To the East Coast.

Someone turned on a light in a window on the other side of the street. I stared at the gap between the curtains. A woman was feeding a baby. It wasn't that she couldn't sleep. She was just feeding the baby. I checked the time on my phone. It was after midnight.

I lay down wearing just my boxers. It was hot in the room and the pillow pressed uncomfortably into the back of my neck. How many people had slept in this bed? I sank into the soft mattress. There were hundreds of bodies beneath me. Naked. Intertwined. Arms, legs, hair. I began to feel short of breath, but the more I tried to get to the surface, the more I sank into the pile of human bodies. Rotting debris, decomposing remains. Dry particles of skin and protruding white bones. Skulls, buttocks and stomachs pinned me down, pushing me deeper, lower. I wanted to scream, but when I opened my mouth it was immediately filled with the white breasts of dead women. Fat larvae slithered into my nostrils and ears. I tried to shake them out but—

I leaped to my feet. My heart was pounding against my ribcage, I couldn't catch my breath.

In a sweat, I went over to the window. The woman opposite was still feeding her baby. She was sitting with her back to me now. You turned your back to me too when you breastfed her. I was meeting her the next day. I reached into my jacket pocket for my cigarettes and went out into the hallway.

That day, the day I met you, I was standing in the stairway smoking. I was last but one in the queue for an oral exam with your father.

He received us in his office in pairs. He got up from behind the desk, buttoned his jacket, smoothed his hair. Thinning on the top of his head. A handshake. Have a seat, gentlemen. Please select your questions.

Three wooden chairs, a broken cabinet, empty inside, a desk on spindly legs, a large medieval window on the left-hand side with a view of the town hall. A narrow, tarnished mirror hung on the opposite wall. What for? Probably to mock us, so that we could see our own futility.

I was sweating like a pig. My shirt clung to my back, sweat collected in drops on my upper lip. I was scared that he'd stand up and hold out his hand to me—thank you, that's all—so I kept wiping my hands on my thighs so that I'd be ready. But I wasn't ready. He surprised me anyway.

'I have plans for you,' he announced.

I took a breath, and he continued, 'Come and see me sometime.'

And there was his hand. I didn't have time to wipe mine on my trousers. I was dying of shame for having such a sticky, wet hand, and he was still holding it, saying, 'See you soon.'

Out in the corridor, my friend and I checked our marks. I'd passed. I'd more than passed. He'd invited me for a meeting. Me, not my friend.

'Why you? You're no eminent scholar, not even a particularly good one!'

In a single moment I'd made a switch—losing a friend and gaining a patron. Why me? Me, no eminent scholar, not even a particularly good one.

True, this was the sort of offer everyone wished for in their heart of hearts. An invitation to meet with the professor, lively discussions, meaningful silences indicating respect for your interlocutor, an outstanding dissertation written with his guidance, leading to a PhD and his office door always being open, and eventually a dazzling legal career. Everyone. Including me.

I stubbed out my cigarette against the wall. There were no ashtrays. I went back to my hotel room. I lay down on the bed, afraid to fall asleep.

I went to see him in the evenings. He'd give me a legal dilemma to solve, and as I sat in his office with my shirt clinging to my back and sweat sliding down between my buttocks, he'd circle around me in his overly tight jacket. He'd pace back and forth. He'd stand behind me and rock on his feet, heel-toe, heel-toe. I could see him in the mirror hanging on the wall. I'd steal surreptitious glances. So would he. He'd breathe calmly just above my ear. He'd put his hand on my shoulder. I'd feel its weight. I felt his weight on me.

I turned over on to my other side.

I really was an average student. I always arrived for his class at the last minute. I sat by the door. Or by the stove, which was advantageous in winter. He stood at the lectern and spoke without interruption for ninety minutes. I didn't raise my head, I pretended to be diligently taking notes. And he was speaking to me. I felt it. Sometimes he came out from behind the lectern and circled the room. He stood behind me, looked over my shoulder, I knew he was reading my notes. Then slowly, the floorboards creaking under his shoes, slowly, he returned to his lectern, not interrupting his lecture for even a second.

The pillow was pressing into my throat. I had to change position.

In the spring, a fly awoke between the windowpanes in the lecture hall and started up a monotonous buzzing. The more I tried to ignore it, the more clearly I heard it. Its buzz echoed in my head, I felt I was going crazy. But it kept buzzing. The entire windowpane trembled, the windowsill, the wall, the whole university. The world was shaken to its core.

The lecture was on the legitimacy of law.

The floor creaked again. He came down from his lectern, walked slowly, slid between the desks, bent over me and reached above my head. His armpit was half an inch from my face. I could smell his strong aftershave. He was silent for a moment. He took my notebook and carefully squashed the fly with it. He pressed it with his finger. It burst with a pop. A sound I really did not want to hear, but I heard very clearly. Poof. Poof and it's gone. A spurt of white eggs. There was silence in the room. Dead silence, you might say. The floorboards creaked and he returned to his place. He continued his lecture. I wanted to take notes, but I couldn't. The fly's white larvae were stuck to my notebook.

I never used it again, I bought a new one.

I lay down facing the window. The light from over the road shone in my eyes. Is that woman still breastfeeding? My boxers had ridden up between my cheeks and were squashing my balls. I tried to take them off, but I got tangled in the hotel sheet. It was stuffy and hot. The radiators were on full blast. They ought to lower the temperature at night. I went to the bathroom.

When I left the lecture hall I went straight to the toilets. He came in a second later. He went for the urinal on the left. He didn't look in my direction. I didn't look in his direction either, but out of the corner of my eye I saw we were undoing our flies at the same time, we took out our penises with the same movement, put our left hands against the wall the same way, at the same height. I tried to hold back, to avoid letting out a stream before he did. I couldn't stand the tension. With relief, I noted that we were pissing at the same time. We finished together. Intuitively, we shook off the last few drops and both pressed the flush with our elbows. We did up our trousers. We went to wash our hands. There was only one sink. I let him go first. There was no soap and no towel. I noticed that he reluctantly held just the ends of his fingers under the stream of water and hurriedly turned off the tap. If I hadn't been looking at his hands, he wouldn't have washed them at all. He pushed the door handle to open the door.

'Thank you, Professor. See you soon,' I said, avoiding eye contact.

He turned in the doorway.

'My pleasure,' he said with a smile. He didn't respond to my 'see you soon'.

I went over to the window. The Alfa Romeo, with its leather upholstery, was parked down below. The light had gone out in the building opposite. I was still afraid to fall asleep.

What was I thanking him for?

'How did you meet her?'

'Who?' I answered a question with a question.

My daughter was standing in front of me, looking so like you that when I saw her today, twenty-five years later, coming into the café, looking around, taking off her gloves, brushing a wisp of hair behind her ear, I had no doubt that it was you. Sorry. That it was her.

'I fancy a smoke,' she said a moment later, playing with her coffee cup.

I reach into my pocket and take out a pack of Camels. No ashtray. We have to go outside. She wraps her shawl around her and puts on her thin leather gloves. Her hand adorned with soft leather reminds me of something.

'Aren't you cold?' I ask, lighting her cigarette.

I'm standing in the freezing cold in my suit jacket. It's starting to snow. Between the historic Pod Murzynami tenement building (what I wouldn't give to live there!) and the Kraków Cloth Hall sits an old-fashioned carriage. Two horses are stamping their hooves against the cobbles of the main square. A Japanese couple are taking a selfie. A single bell rings out from St Mary's Basilica, half past—

'How did you two meet?'

'Who?'

'How did you meet Mum?'

'How? Me? In the usual way.' I catch her eye. I've said the wrong thing. 'It was spring 1982. Your mother had just come back from... God, where had she come back from?'

'When?'

'When we met. She came to a department meeting, sat down next to the dean. I even remember her dress, charcoal-grey, almost black. She was presenting a paper on seventeenth-century torture devices. She made an impression on me.'

'With the torture devices?'

I burst out laughing, rather unnaturally, to show her that I felt completely at ease.

'No.'

'How, then?'

I'd finished my cigarette and was looking around for a bin. With the tip of her shoe she nudged her fag end through the drain grating. Just like her mother used to.

'What about you? How do you spend your time?' she'd asked.

'Me? I'm a collector.'

'Of what?'

'Maps.' I wanted to be original.

'In that case, after the meeting I'll show you what I've brought from the Jesuit library in Heidelberg,' she said.

'What do you mean, how?'

'How did she make an impression on you?'

God, I don't know.

'God, I don't know,' I said.

'Are you done smoking? Let's go in.'

Dusk began to fall. The meeting started at 6 p.m. on a Thursday.

She came in, looked around the room, adjusted the black lock of hair on her forehead. She sat down next to the dean.

She came in and the sight of her overwhelmed me.

She came in, and it was you.

I rose slightly from my chair so that she'd recognise me. The relief on her face. The tension on her father's face. His heavy hand on my thigh brought me back to my seat. I felt like a horse being held back before a race.

'After the meeting we'll discuss your final grades,' he whispered.

His breath was sweet and sour. He smelled of fermented apples and the smoke of burnt meadows. As his daughter talked about torture devices, he played with his fountain pen with the arrowhead nib. His dark-green pen. His pen that lay beautifully in his hand. That, despite its size and weight, twirled nimbly between his fingers. Between fingers with short, square, thickened nails. Between fingers with knuckles covered in coarse black hair. Coarse, black hair.

What was I thanking him for?

'Are you done smoking? Let's go in,' she said.

I held the door open for her.

The waiter came over.

'What are you drinking, honey?'

'Whatever you're having,' she replied.

Is that a joke? Was that a joke?

'Two coffees and...' I hesitated, then continued, 'two cognacs.'

The galloping of my thoughts must have been audible. What does she do? Who is she? What should I ask her about? And what if the topics of conversation suddenly dry up?

'Do you even know what I do? Did Mum tell you?'

I shook my head.

'No. We talked about—'

I made a vague hand gesture. She knew what we'd talked about. She must have known. She closed her eyes for a split second longer than a normal blink. Of course! There was nothing more to—

The waiter brought the cognac.

'And the coffee?'

'Right away.'

My eyes followed him as he left the room.

For what seemed like an eternity, we were silent.

'Your coffee.' The waiter seemed to pity us as he bent over the table.

She adjusted her jumper, crossed one leg over the other. The coffee.

'Do you take sugar?'

'What?! Me?'

I didn't take sugar either. The first sip was hideous. How could anyone drink this reeking, pitch-black, burnt paste?

'Amazing, isn't it? This coffee is the reason I come here. It's Ethiopian.'

'Ethiopian.' I nodded knowledgably. 'Yes.' I took a sip of cognac to kill the taste of the dregs on my tongue. I was about to launch into 'In my day…', but I took another sip of the Ethiopian to revive my mind and fell silent. Fuck, I really want to smoke, yelled my mind, but I told it to pipe down.

'So how did you two meet?' she asks, breaking the silence.

'Who?' I answer a question with a question.

Her ring finger traces the rim of her glass. She hasn't touched her cognac. She takes it in her hand, warms it, smells it, puts it down. She looks around the room, then back at the amber liquid in the glass. She plays with her coffee cup.

'I fancy a smoke.'

I reach into my pocket and take out the pack of Camels. No ashtray. We have to go outside. She wraps her shawl around her and puts on her thin leather gloves. Her hand adorned with soft leather.

'Aren't you cold in those?' I ask, lighting her cigarette. Déjà vu.

Everyone has their secrets. When I was afraid I'd fall asleep, I'd get up and stand to attention. I stood to attention because I was afraid I'd fall asleep. I was afraid of that dream.

The wind rattled the bare branches. Over and over again, the black birds took flight and circled, circled, circled above the square with the well in the middle. A dog was sitting at my side. If I stretched out the fingers of my left hand, I could touch its head. I didn't have to. I knew it was there. I was the man, I was the other one, I was the dog. My eyes were closed. I could see everything.

I stood with my eyes closed. I was wearing black boots and leather gloves. I'll never forget how soft they were inside. Now and then, I moved my finger to evoke that feeling, to consciously experience the touch of the inside of the leather glove. And although I was standing with my face towards the bright rays of the sun, my attention was drawn to the dark interior of the leather adorning my hand. The sun emerged from behind the clouds for a moment. The flock of black birds circled again. I stood with my eyes closed, warming my face.

And he ordered me to select all the white, pregnant ones. So I gathered them together and lined them up on the square next to the well. They waited, bare and swollen. They were already shaved. He examined them one by one.

My eyes were closed. I tried with all my strength not to open them, but I still saw and knew everything. They walked, one behind the other, and they looked at me. The more they looked at me, the more I hated them.

I wanted to wake up, but it was impossible. If you're not sleeping, you can't wake up.

I led them to the courtyard, near the well. They were large and lumbering. Their eyes were sleepy, unaccustomed to the sunlight. They crowded together.

'It's important that they're alive when you open them up. It's the young I want. If you damage any skin, you'll pay with your own,' he said.

A strong gust of wind carried a sweet smell of smoke. It was autumn.

I didn't speak. I took a rope, tied them up one at a time and cut open their stomachs. The sky, the clouds and the flock of black birds reflected in the blade of my knife again and again. I slashed the taut skin on their bellies and extracted the bloodstained young. I plunged them immediately into a bucket of water, held their heads under just long enough. Not too long, not too short. When the water grew thick and dark, I drew fresh, cold, clean water from the well. I changed it seven times. And he stood with his eyes closed, his face raised towards the sun.

They waited all day for their turn. Vacant, sleepy. The longer they waited, the more I felt hatred towards them. I wanted them to suffer. I wanted them to know what would happen to them. And I wanted them to know that it was me. Me. But they were too stupid to understand.

It took all day. The heap of dead ewes grew on one side, an orderly pile of snow-white lambs on the other. I counted them all. They were worth their weight in gold.

I stood to attention in the hotel room because I was afraid to fall asleep. The light from the street lamp filtered through the window. The neatly parked car was down below.

You could see the cathedral from the window. His car was down below.

'Two hundred and four fails, three Cs, two Bs, one B plus,' I reported.

'Stay away from her.' He said it only once.

I couldn't stay away from her. Not any more. Every evening, she stood in front of me naked in our junior staff accommodation. And I reached between her legs, which she spread for me obediently. She was so submissive. With her right hand she guided me between her labia, parting them with her left hand. Sometimes they were dry and I had to moisten them with my tongue in order to—

Or she would kneel before me and I felt like a god between her lips. Her lips were always moist. Or I would kneel behind her and she would dutifully offer up her buttocks. And then I couldn't see her face.

I couldn't stay away from her. Just like I couldn't get closer.

'Your ear is like a snowflake,' I whispered from behind. I couldn't hear her words. I heard her spasmodic breathing. Which could easily be mistaken for despair.

'We need to talk,' she said. She laid her hands on the café table. The waiter served the coffee in tall glasses. 'The doctor said it's due in March.'

We said nothing. It was late. Too late.

She broke the silence—'What will happen with us?'—and I told her everything would be OK. She replied that her father might cause us some trouble.

'Why would he?' I asked.

'Because he loved you, you were—'

'We weren't in love.'

'—his favourite student. I didn't say you were in love. I said you were his favourite student.'

What was I thanking him for? I had nothing to thank him for.

'Were you?'

Before Christmas she went home to get her things. All she cared about was the map she'd acquired on her scholarship year in Heidelberg. She'd brought it back as a souvenir.

'A souvenir of what?' I joked, but she didn't get it. She raised her black eyes to me. And she looked at me like the time when—

I stood across the street and waited for her. I wasn't allowed to set foot in that house any more, so I paced up and down on the pavement that the Kraków townspeople had built after 500 years. My feet were frozen, I was out of cigarettes. And that's when he signed his name on the will in which—

All she cared about was getting that map from sometime in the fifteenth century, a map drawn in gold shavings on the finest parchment made from the skin of lambs extracted from the stomachs of live mothers, drawn by an unparalleled cartographer who had been banished to a Camaldolese monastery and spent the rest of his life far away from everything he loved. I had seen that map once in my life and I could never forget it. Then she came out of the house with a box of books and a radio, but no map.

'After he dies. I'll get it after he dies,' she said. 'Not until he's dead.'

And her eyes darkened with anger. And she looked at me like—

I lay in my hotel room. I was afraid to fall asleep. I stared at the ceiling. I said, 'Then the divorce will cost you half the inheritance,' and you said nothing, you just looked at me for what seemed like an eternity. Like back then. The first tram rolled past on the street. The ground shook. I went over to the window to close the blinds. The Alfa Romeo was there waiting. I leaned on the windowsill. The sky was brightening in the east. I was afraid of that dream.

I stood bent over the map and gazed at the image of this world, and despair came over me. In an instant, the half-breath between being delivered from evil and being led into temptation, I felt it was all emptiness. There's nothing to fight for. All is lost. A whole life spent creating a map of the world from gold shavings, a world that no king, no pope, no God needed. On the finest parchment made from the skin of white lambs taken from live mothers, on parchment worthy of the high and mighty of this world, on this parchment we drew a map with gold dust, Fra Mauro and I, for which he wanted to buy salvation, and I freedom. Salvation that doesn't exist. Freedom that doesn't exist. Temptation.

I was seized with despair because my whole life seemed a mistake. They said I was seeking hell. They were wrong. I carried hell inside me.

I have lost my way, Lord, I whispered through pale lips. I have lost my way. I, the great sailor, the traveller, the immortal cartographer. I, the navigator. I. Allow me, Lord, to return once again to the raging oceans, to approach the distant shore, and I will concoct for You a hell that You could never dream of. Just let me return.

I drew for God a map of hell. I drew it with golden sand. I drew for days and nights. I was afraid I would fall asleep.

When I had finished, I rolled up the parchment and slid it into a long tube lined with red velvet. I told Giovanni Boldù to keep it safe.

Until the time came.

The sea roared with the rising tide. Packs of hungry dogs were waiting at the harbour. I was ready. I was just waiting for Giovanni. When his thick, stocky frame finally appeared against the starlit sky, I went to call out to him, I raised my hand, but suddenly I felt a pain in the back of my head and blood was pouring into my mouth. Someone was stamping my face into the wooden planks of the walkway. Then there was darkness.

The black sky opened up above the clouds. The flight went smoothly. I'd been in the US for New Year's. With some embarrassment, I'd acknowledged that my girlfriend was a few months younger than my daughter. I hadn't realised it before. In some ways it made my life complicated, but everything went back to normal when I simply changed women.

My divorce hearing was set for May. I landed at Warsaw Chopin Airport. The city smelled of lilacs.

I was due to meet my wife on the Tuesday after I landed to discuss the details, but a lawyer showed up in her place—Hubert van Severin, grandson of Hermann van Severin, from Antwerp, thirty-five years old, in a well-tailored suit and Doc Martens. His lightly tanned face (skiing in Switzerland?) was graced with well-groomed facial hair and a boyish smile. From his clear complexion, I gathered he had a healthy digestive system.

'My client has asked me to stand in for her.' His bright eyes left me in no doubt: first, he was telling the truth; second, that was all the information I'd be getting.

I said nothing.

He maintained the silence for a short time, and then said, 'Here's a proposal for the contract,' and presented a folder of documents showing that after the divorce she would claim the full inheritance, then she would pay me half the value of any property we had acquired jointly during our marriage. We had not acquired any property jointly during our marriage.

I smiled. This proposal was unacceptable.

'I have no objections. I'll accept the proposal in full, of course,' I said. 'Just allow me to clarify. With regards to the items that constitute the estate. Let's say they were acquired during the marriage.'

Hubert van Severin took the documents from me.

'Such findings would be inconsistent with the facts.'

'So let's make them consistent. It's simpler than it seems. My wife would just need to claim the inheritance before the divorce.'

The boyish smile, his bright-blue eyes sparkling.

'I'm sorry. My client is unable to claim the inheritance before the divorce. Her father made it clear in his will that she would be his only heir, on the condition that she was not your wife. We are interpreting this bequest very generously, actually, in allowing the divorce. But… But for certain reasons, we don't have much time.'

I didn't ask the question that was on the tip of my tongue.

He closed the folder, stood and buttoned up his jacket. I stood too. We walked to the door. A manly handshake. Boyish smile, bright gaze.

'I thought Mum told you.'

My daughter was standing in front of me, tugging at the strap of her handbag. Her skin was covered in freckles and had taken on a warm shade of tan. If she put on a charcoal-grey dress, she'd look like you. But no. First of all, she was taller. Second, she was wearing jeans.

'What?'

'What do you mean, what?'

'Told me what?'

'You said you'd talked and she told you, back then, in December.'

'No. I mean, yes. We talked. But didn't she tell you?'

'I've known from the start. I was the first to see the results.'

'What results?'

'Histopathology. Didn't she tell you anything?'

'We talked about—'

We talked about money. About the divorce and the inheritance.

'Where is she now?'

'In a hospital in Bydgoszcz. He works there, her—'

She broke off. Her what?

'And what if we don't get divorced? Who'll be the heir?' I asked Hubert van Severin, without the unnecessary preliminaries, the moment he picked up the phone.

'Hello, Andrzej. I was waiting for you to ask that. I understand that a divorce might not seem like the right thing. However, if my client is unable to claim the inheritance, the next in line will be the deceased's brother. His monastery has shown a keen interest in the inheritance proceedings. A cardinal has even been appointed to monitor the case. After all, the potential heir is of advanced age. We don't have much time.'

The Alfa Romeo took the corners smoothly. The miles flew by. I rested my left hand on the steering wheel, with my right I touched the gear stick again and again, making sure I was in fifth. I wasn't tired. I'd left just after midnight, but it was almost the shortest night of the year and the darkness soon gave way to dawn. The sun was rising somewhere behind me, I could see it in my rear-view mirror. I was driving on the motorway. The regular morning traffic was beginning to appear. I didn't stop for a coffee until Heidelberg. In the foothills leading to the monastery where her father's brother was spending his old age. *His* brother.

Before they let me in, I had to answer a few difficult questions about the family tree, fill out a form and sign it.

I followed a young monk in a white habit down a long, bright corridor. He led me up some stairs to the first floor. He told me that *his* brother—my father-in-law's brother, my wife's uncle, my daughter's great-uncle—had been confined to his bed for a long time now. He lay there with his face as pale as wax, his hands clasped. Every day he received the sacraments, he said the Litany of the Sacred Heart of Jesus, he ate a warm meal. But he no longer recognised his confrères, he had no sense of time, was less and less connected with earthly life, ever closer to the light eternal.

'How nice that you came all the way from America to say goodbye. We would have informed you about his death and the funeral anyway, although his only family, since he took his religious vows, is that of Societas Iesu,' said the young monk.

I nodded to show that I understood.

The window of his cell looked out on to the monastery garden. The sun came in at an angle, forming a bright diamond on the side wall where the high medical bed stood. He lay covered with a sheet. His eyes were open, his gaze fixed on the ceiling. I stepped closer. He didn't move an inch. What was I expecting? That he'd tell me about himself and about—

And about *him*? That he'd look like *him*? He didn't. I touched his hand. His fingers were long and thin, his nails pink and almond-shaped. He didn't look like *him*. He was completely different.

The young monk stood in the doorway. He turned his head discreetly, but he stayed inside the cell.

I left. My visit lasted three minutes.

'The cells of the oldest monks are here in this corridor. We call it "the runway",' said the young monk with a playful glint in his eye as we walked back the way we came.

I smiled in response.

When I got outside, it was midday. I was hungry. I stopped at the nearest restaurant and ate a heavy lunch. I felt like having a beer, but I had to get back. I took an Americano to go. I had a couple of sips in the car park. It tasted like tepid dishwater. I left it by the bin. I tore out of the car park a bit too quickly, the tyres screeching at the bend. Within a few minutes I was on the motorway, heading east. Drowsiness came over me unexpectedly. I was afraid I'd fall asleep. With all the effort I could muster, I concentrated on driving, but after Nuremberg I took the wrong exit. Instead of Dresden I was heading for Leipzig. I didn't want to turn around. Five hours later I was in Frankfurt. I stopped to get petrol. There was a brief rain shower around six in the evening. The air smelled of wet asphalt. I rested both hands on the steering wheel. I turned on the radio. Which of the Bydgoszcz hospitals was she in?

Two cars were parked on the forecourt outside the hospital.

A nurse in heavy make-up informed me that the May bank holiday weekend was just starting, so there were no doctors I could talk to about my wife's condition, and that visiting hours had ended at eight. I looked at my watch. It was almost nine.

'I've come from the US to see her,' I said, and in a way it was true. She looked at me through eyelashes thick with mascara.

'OK, but there's really no point. Anyway,' she came out from behind the reception desk to direct me, 'anyway, you'll see.'

She walked in front of me. Her tight blue tunic enveloped an unbelievably tiny bum. We entered the staff lift. There were no numbers on the panel, just abbreviations. PAL. ICU. OB-GYN. OAP. Orthotics and Prosthetics?

The lift opened and we took a left. I wouldn't be able to find my way back. I noticed that we passed a chapel along the way. A huge, dark cross on an empty wall. I thought I saw a monk praying on a prie-dieu, but when I looked again there was no one there.

'Your wife is in a medically induced coma. Her condition is stable,' the nurse said, holding the door open for me.

Dusk fell. A large chestnut tree was blossoming outside the window. Its white flowers reflected the light coming from below, making it look like they were emitting their own glow.

I went over to her bed. Her eyes were closed and her face peaceful. Pink, almond-shaped fingernails. I didn't have the courage to touch her, so I adjusted her quilt, to mark my presence in some way. So that the kindness of the nurse with the tiny bum didn't go to waste. I turned, but she wasn't at the door. She wasn't standing where she should have been. I'd been left alone. One on one. The respirator whirred quietly. The dot on the electrocardiograph machine plotted an endless faint chart. The chestnut flowers shone with an inner light. I left the room, closing the door behind me.

She was standing in the corridor leaning against a windowsill.

'Well? Didn't I tell you?'

We passed the dark chapel on the way back. A feeling of meaninglessness came over me. It was as though the battle was still raging, but there was nothing left to fight for. I couldn't breathe. I had to undo my shirt collar.

We took the lift down to the ground floor and I went out through the wide glass doors. A warm May wind swept over me in the car park. It brought the scent of chestnut flowers and something else.

I got into the car. Its elegant leather interior offered a precarious sense of comfort. I was afraid, terribly afraid, that I'd fall asleep.

The Map

My father loved maps. He adored maps. He owned maps. He collected maps. His study was lined with glass cabinets specially designed for storing maps. Inside were long tubes intended exclusively for maps. And wide, shallow drawers which, of course, held—

Was there anything my father wouldn't do to obtain a desired object, a longed-for original, a draft, an incunable? Hard to say. Today, though, now that I'm an old man, my shoulders trembling beneath my purple overcoat—today, kneeling at night in the hospital chapel, I don't think so. I don't think there was anything. I cover my face with my hands and feel a sob rising in my throat. I understand, I really do understand his desire.

I was seven years old when I first set foot in my father's study. This honour was granted to me in March 1953, in Hoboken on the outskirts of Antwerp. Oh, I was not aware then of the existence of east and west—at that time, I still thought the sun revolved around the earth. On the day of my seventh birthday, I remember.

Entering the study was strictly forbidden.

Impossible, even, because the study was ruthlessly protected, locked with a key, a single key which my father, Adolf Alois Adler, always carried with him in a leather wallet, along with documents and banknotes, in his inner jacket pocket.

Without the key, entering the study was impossible.

It wasn't possible then. Only later, a few years later, through the window that caught the sunlight, along the black beam of the timber-framed wall, over which the sun crept just before dying on the horizon—when the desire to touch my father's maps became unbearable. So along this beam, slanting, running from the never-cleaned attic window to the window of the study, along this perfectly sloping beam, corresponding to the rays of the setting sun, along this black beam it was possible to enter the study without permission. But only a few years later.

So I was seven years old when I first entered the study of my father, Adolf Alois Adler; I was his only heir.

'You can take a look around, boy. Just, for God's sake, don't touch anything,' he said.

I didn't touch.

I could count to ten: five cabinets on one wall, five on the other. A small picture between the windows. Black and white. An old man leaning over a glowing map, his head turned at an angle. Terror in his eyes. Did I glimpse a sudden movement, a shake of his birdlike head?

'The non-existent *Faust*,' said Father casually. 'Etching.'

Etching. I thought it was the artist's name. Lucky I didn't say anything! I just stood with my hands clasped behind me, so as not to touch.

Many years later, in order to get an estimate for the inheritance, I had the artwork appraised. It was by no means the most valuable piece in my father's collection, but it was indeed an unknown etching by Rembrandt. It wasn't until a few years later that I heard that name.

So, I'm in my father's study. In the middle, a desk. Black, with drawers. Father takes a street map from one of the drawers and lays it out on the desk.

'Don't touch it,' he repeats, and opens one of the cabinets.

Out of the corner of my eye I see him unroll a scroll of dry parchment made of paper-thin leather. A scroll of parchment with a map of the world drawn in pure gold shavings. A world accessible only to sailors and travellers, troublemakers and outlaws condemned to eternal exile. Men. I was not yet a man then.

So, while my father slides the map from its dark tube, I lean in over the city map. Closer. I can see a wide street between three-storey tenement buildings. A tramline. A tram leaving the station. Signboards. Kowalsky & Abrahamsohn, Palast-Café, Bromberg—I spell them out.

I stand with my hands clasped behind my back and look down at Danzigerstrasse—no, sorry, it was a sunny day in September, seven years before I was born, a Friday—Adolfstrasse. I stand and I look, hands clasped behind my back. I don't touch anything. To reach the town hall, you have to take big, long strides. I know where to go. I know this street, I know this square. Wrought-iron gate, wide steps. The creak of black patent-leather boots. I push the door open with my shoulder. I go inside.

A cool, stone interior. To get to the records (why the records? I'm more interested in the archive, archives are in basements!), you have to run up to the first floor. I run. Then you go to the end of the corridor and take a right. It's the last door on the left. I go inside.

A long, narrow room. Brown cabinets, each bearing a catalogue number and letter of the alphabet. A double window at the end. Geraniums on the windowsill. I walk over, hands clasped behind my back. I look down at the square. Lots of men in uniforms and shiny black boots. The monument to the man with no horse and the two towers of the Jesuit church. Hirsch's café on the left-hand side. I decide I'll go there for a coffee later, and I ask to see the relevant documents.

A woman in a dark-grey dress, hair pinned in an intricate chignon, gives me everything I ask for. Documents, maps, plans. I look at the yellowed pages, read the names of people and places written in a difficult, rustling Slavic language. Left hand still behind my back, the right hand in its black leather glove turns the dry pages. I don't recognise it. I don't know who it belongs to. Is it mine?

'*Was ist das?*' I ask in a voice that's not my own.

'It's a map of a non-existent city,' says my father just above my ear.

I turn my head towards him and, for a moment, I'm seven years old again.

'This city does not exist,' repeats Adolf Alois Adler, tapping with a yellowed fingernail as crooked as a bird's claw on the black desktop where the map is laid out, a map made in copying pencil, dated 1912 and inscribed with the title 'Bromberg' in Gothic lettering, and in the lower-right-hand corner…

'The first draft of Stübben's plan, never realised. A rare item,' he adds, bending down to one of the lower shelves of the black, glass-fronted map cabinet.

I lean over Hermann Joseph Stübben's map, staring at the non-existent crossroads, the buildings that aren't there, the ruins of the Jesuit church. A cloud of birds obscures the setting sun; for a moment, it goes dark. I look up. With a sharp, sudden movement, Father turns his head towards the window and in this instant he looks like Faust, like the Faust from the picture on the wall. I can see his eagle-like face. Jesus!

But he's already slipped Stübben's map into the desk drawer. He wanted to show me something else.

'On your tenth birthday, I'll give you this map, son,' he said, laying out in front of me a large, dry parchment with an upside-down map of the world. 'On your tenth birthday,' he repeated, and I counted quickly on my fingers, that's three years, Dad, that day will never come. Have mercy, Father, don't condemn me to eternal suffering; but I said simply, 'Yes, Father.'

And I stood, looked, and touched nothing.

Then Father rolled it back up, slipped it into the dark, soft opening of the tube lined with red velvet and closed the lid. He crouched down and laid it on the shelf second from bottom, where there was no glass in the doors so even the begrudging rays of the setting sun couldn't reach, couldn't peek, couldn't covet Fra Mauro's map, the lost map that Mauro created in 1455 in a monastery in southern Europe.

Father turned to face me and nodded towards the door. I left the room.

I inherited from my mother the shape of her mouth, a predilection for the Polish language and an aversion to black birds. I remember Mum always wore black dresses with long sleeves, even in August. When the maid hung them on the clothes line, they flapped in the wind like ravens' wings. I guess I was afraid of them.

Six months later, in early autumn, I broke the blue milk jug and everyone in the house started crying. I was scared of my father's reaction, so I went to the kitchen, to the cook, and said, 'I've broken Mum's blue jug.'

But she started crying too, she hugged me, buried my face in her bosom and whispered, 'Poor child, what'll happen to us now.'

I didn't think the jug was that important. Nonetheless, I felt extremely guilty and responsible for the death of my mother, who had been cleaning the attic window that morning (so my nanny told me, and so everyone said later on, although Mum didn't clean windows, I'd never seen her cleaning windows, and no one ever cleaned that attic window, no one even opened it, but I didn't tell them that, I just nodded), yes, that very morning Mum was standing on the window ledge in her black dress and the wind had tossed her to the ground. It was a fatal fall. I hoped that it had nothing to do with the jug, but I was scared that in fact it did. I bore that feeling of guilt alone until my first confession, when Father Nathaniel gave me absolution.

My father met my mother a year before I was born, when she was travelling north from Esterwegen. That's all I know. No documents, witnesses, family mementoes. Nothing. Apparently, she'd brought with her a cookbook, the blue milk jug, and the picture that hung in my father's study. It was the only picture that hung in his study. I remember she was a beautiful woman, she spoke to me in Polish and German, she sang lullabies and kissed me on the forehead. Sometimes I thought she had black hair, other times fair. I guess it depended on the light.

In any case, now that I'm an old man, the image of my mother, whom I last saw on a Sunday evening when she kissed me goodnight, and after breakfast I smashed that wretched jug, and from then on everyone who looked at me nodded and said, 'Ah, poor Adrian, his mother…' and patted my head or gave me sweets—that image has become somewhat blurred. The black dress. That I remember clearly. How old was I then? Seven and a half?

There was always a nanny at our house in Hoboken, Antwerp, northern Flanders. They can't all have been called Nanny, but I never learned any of their real names. I never asked. They washed, cooked, played with me and told scary stories. One was old and wore a wide apron tied at the waist. She was the one who tended to my mother's dresses and she was the one who pressed my head to her bosom that day so tightly that I could hardly breathe. But a year later there was another one, and then another. And they all made coffee for my father and hot chocolate for me. And they always wanted something from me. Usually for me to eat up, or hurry up.

One of them taught me to read, but I don't know which. That was when Mum was still alive. I remember that she was alive because when I announced to Father that I could read, he said disapprovingly, 'All literature is just an endless combination of twenty-odd letters, nothing more.'

And she said, 'Leave him be.'

My father just shook his head and shot me a scathing glance.

I guess that was the moment I stopped valuing literature, permanently and irrevocably; a few months later, on my seventh birthday in March 1953, leaning over the desk upon which was spread the map of the non-existent city of Bromberg, I understood the value of graphic depictions of reality. Or at least, conceptions of reality. From that moment on, my desire to enter my father's study grew stronger. He had promised, after all.

The tight jacket and too-short trousers. That I remember. I always had long limbs, but at the age of ten, when my mother had been dead almost three years, and Father had hired yet another nanny, all my clothes were too small for me. I felt like a puppet, marching behind Adolf Alois Adler up the wide staircase to the second floor and down the dark hallway.

Father leaning over, the arc of his back—I can see it even now, how he stood slightly to the side to let in some light, while I—I remember clearly, I'm crying out in my soul: now, now, now, Dad! He pushes the door open with his shoulder and I follow him into the study. The room is bathed in the last rays of the sun; God, how beautiful!

Father lays out a large drawing board, brown, smelling of varnish. But that's not important! As he reaches into the cabinet and unfurls the huge map of the world on material so dry and thin it could disintegrate at any moment, I open the drawer and breathe in the smell of Stübben's map; I don't even touch it, just close my eyes and...

Night.

Night. Hospital. The smell of Lysol. The moonlight seeping through the blossoming branches of the chestnut tree. The whir of the breathing apparatus, the regular rhythm of the heartbeat. I see everything. The clock on the wall, it's nearly four, shadows on the floor, the white chair, the white bed, the woman's white body. Is she sleeping? I get closer. Medical history. This is her medical history. All those letters, but I don't understand them, I don't understand them yet. I look at her. Who is she? She's opening her eyes, Jesus!

In an instant, I return to the map that Father...

Now that I'm an old man, I think my body has places just like that parchment on which Fra Mauro drew the world, giving shape to the stories of the sailors, travellers, troublemakers and murderers who wound up in the Port of Venice in 1447. I know such places exist on the human body.

'Look, this is the man who drew the map.' Father holds out a medal in his palm.

'*Cosmographus incomparabilis*,' I read out loud.

Ugly, I think.

'Hold it. See how heavy it is,' he says.

My gaze escapes to the window. The blossoming branches of the chestnut tree. It wasn't March. It must have been May already.

In May 1466, Giovanni Boldù stood in his studio and examined the profile of Fra Mauro on the medal he had just made. He felt a growing anger towards the wrinkles of the face and the creases of the monk's cowl. Ugly, he thought. A monster.

What was the point in naming a monk *cosmographus incomparabilis*, casting medals and making all this fuss over nothing, he wondered. He felt dissatisfied with himself, the meaninglessness of his work and the worthlessness of the cartographer. But he'd done the job because that's what he was paid for, and you don't turn your nose up at commissions like that. Giovanni Boldù did business with traders from Mainz and Kairouan, and he'd often seen Fra Mauro, clad in his white Camaldolese cloak, talking to the sailors. He bought them alcohol in the taverns and paid with jingling coins. He was followed everywhere by another man, Andreas—younger, with a gloomy face and raven-black hair, his eyes always darting from side to side. It was said that he had once been a sailor himself, but his uncle had cut off his funds. Fra Mauro and Andreas talked to the people in the port and met at Hirsch's inn in the evenings, but it didn't look like they were doing the usual work of monks. It really didn't.

When Andreas Bianco first walked into Giovanni's studio, he didn't inspire confidence, but he put a pouch down on the table and left, and Giovanni understood that from then on, he would prepare twice as many parchments as the Camaldolese monastery ordered. That was how they met. On one parchment, Fra Mauro drew the entire world. For the King of Spain, and for his money. On a second parchment, Andreas was to make a secret copy for his uncle, the King of Portugal, for his money. How did Giovanni make the parchment? Everyone has their secrets.

Several years later, Andreas pushed open the low door of Giovanni's studio once again and said in an unpleasant, birdlike voice, 'You're going to make me a tube, six feet long, a handsbreadth wide. And line it with red velvet.'

Giovanni neither spoke nor moved. What was the point, when it was clear that such customers were not to be refused?

I knew where we were from before Father showed me a map of the world. We came from Germania, it was evident from our features and surname. But for several hundred years our family barely left Flanders. My father left Antwerp briefly in the autumn of 1939, and then for longer in 1943. He spent the rest of his life here, as a doctor. His father's father, my great-grandfather Jasper Adolf Adler, spent his long life in a similar way, as did my father's father, my grandfather Alois Jasper Adler, although his life was short. All of them were educated at Jesuit schools. It was no surprise that the decision was taken, on the Saturday following my tenth birthday, that I would follow in their footsteps. Starting in the new year, I would be schooled within the walls of Societas Iesu.

Looking back now, I can see that it was a good decision, but at the time I was devastated. I'd have done anything not to leave my father's house, still to be able to open the attic window when he was working at the clinic—the window that was never cleaned in the attic—and carefully, step by timid step, to shift along the black slanted beam to the outer ledge of the study window, and, gently lifting one half of the shutter, just enough for the latch to release, jump down quietly on to the floor and be there, inside. Did my father know? Everyone has their secrets.

I was inside. I could do anything. Anything. But I steered clear of the map of the non-existent city of Bromberg, diligently avoided looking at it. I was afraid of that hand in the black leather glove.

I knew where to find the map with Flanders, Germania and Lechia denoted at the bottom, Africa and Asia at the top. The map of the world upside-down. I laid it out on the floor because it didn't fit on the desk. It was over six feet wide. It smelled of a sea breeze, fish and dust. It was dry and thin. I touched. I touched it. I caressed it with my fingertips, combed it with my nails, rubbed my cheek against it. I licked it once, but the trail of my tongue didn't disappear. Then I got scared, I rolled it up hurriedly, slipped it into the soft tube and fled. For the next four or five weeks I didn't go into my father's study, just watched his face vigilantly. And nothing. He didn't notice anything. Perhaps he didn't even look at it all that time. Unbelievable.

Giovanni lived alone. He slept in his studio, ate at Hirsch's, drank wherever he could. A strong wind was blowing off the sea that night. Foul weather. Giovanni was having a bad dream. The shutter banged against the window. He opened his eyes and sat up. His back was covered in cold drops of sweat. Andreas, with his birdlike head, was standing before him in a black cloak. Giovanni could have sworn there were glistening feathers on his forehead. But no. It was just hair, wet from the rain. Andreas slid a roll of parchment into a black tube and said, 'Conceal it well. Hide it away,' and left, closing the door behind him.

From that moment on, the tube with the roll of parchment inside stood leaning against a wall in an alcove in Giovanni's studio. It stood and waited for Andreas to claim it back.

In the spring of 1466, Andreas ordered Giovanni to make a medal with an image of Fra Mauro for his magnate uncle. So it was at the beginning of May that Giovanni raised the red-hot medal into the air and examined Mauro's profile with displeasure. He plunged it into a large bowl of water. A cloud of steam erupted like an evil genie. Giovanni prepared some canvas and a sack. He wrapped up the medal, strapped it to his leg, tucked the long tube under his arm and went out into the narrow street, heading towards the port. Andreas would be waiting for him there. This was two years after Mauro's death.

The sun was just disappearing over the roofs of Venice as Giovanni reached the quay.

After my mum died, the new nanny lived on our floor. The servants' room was occupied by Andreas, known as Ondre, our farmhand. Nanny was ten years older than me, maybe eleven. I don't know exactly. I wasn't spending much time at home then, I was mostly at school or at the monastery. I made friends with Father Nathaniel, who was always eager to talk about the mysteries of faith and religious service. I returned the favour with stories about maps and the inheritance that would one day be mine. We walked around the monastery gardens, sometimes until late at night. I suspect that, for me, Father Nathaniel gave up his evening meals, which I certainly wasn't willing to forgo at the time. When I got home, I invariably went to the kitchen and Nanny, already in her nightgown, would serve me bread and cheese with a cup of hot chocolate. Later, she would come into my room to turn out the light and say, 'Goodnight, Adrian, sleep well, my boy.'

Then she stopped for a moment in the doorway, in the bright streak of light from the corridor, so that her whole body was enveloped in the halo of the white nightgown that reached to her ankles. Then she took a step, I caught a brief glimpse of the space between her thighs, and she closed the door. Eternal darkness fell. I was thirteen years old, nearly fourteen.

I was thirteen years old, nearly fourteen, when my father died.

He died at night in the presence of Nanny, which was a secret. Soon after, a new nanny appeared in our house. A completely different one.

A few days later, I was sitting in the office of my father's friend, the solicitor Hermann van Severin. My hair was combed neatly, my boots shining. He was saying something to me; I was staring at my boots and had a sudden urge to see the non-existent city from Stübben's plan, Bromberg. To wander the streets, see the Jesuit church, enter the town hall and... I wanted it so badly!

'And the key to the study? Did Father leave the key to his study?' I asked in a high, boyish voice.

Hermann van Severin looked at me attentively.

'Yes,' he said. 'Yes, my boy, he left it. Here it is.'

I held out my right palm. I was surprised it wasn't enclosed in the black leather glove that I'd used to slap the woman in the grey dress.

'What the hell? You're hiding German documents from me? You bitch!'

A September afternoon, Bromberg. My God, so many hours within these cold walls, how dull it was. In the corner, leaning against the brick wall, was a long tube with a sealed lid. I was craving coffee and women. We went down to the basement. She, in a grey dress, her hair pinned up, went first; I followed her, my hands clasped behind my back. I only felt the damp and cold of the vaults on my face, but she was shivering. From cold, from fear? The weak light bulb high up in the arches cast more shade than light. The city archives from the sixteenth century. The smell of excitement and adventure. Dust and mould. The female body, and her perfume. In the final contraction of pleasure, I pressed my hand in its black glove to her mouth, she struggled fitfully but didn't make a sound.

I felt dizzy.

'Are you OK, Adrian?' asked the new nanny, and I nodded to show that I was fine, but...

The wooden dock swayed underfoot. Andreas Bianco stood at the end of the pier between the giant hulls of the Moorish ships that had been moored in Venice for three days. He looked around furtively, trying to stay silent. No doubt the crew were yet to return from their libations and brawls. Empty. In the moonlight, a pack of about forty scrawny dogs could be seen running along the waterfront.

'I have what you gave me,' said Giovanni, and the sound of his voice, intensified by the silence, drifted over the rolling water. Andreas said nothing. Did he shake his head slightly? Giovanni took one step towards Andreas, then another.

'Run,' whispered the man who had watched the hands of Fra Mauro, when Mauro was still alive, and who in the silence of the monastery library had drawn his map and a copy comprising the bloody stories of sailors and travellers on which the two of them had fed in the dark haunts around the port. 'Run.'

Two strong hands squashed Andreas's birdlike head against the walkway; a number of heavy feet thudded along in pursuit of Giovanni, who was big and strong, but not fast.

By dawn on 4 May 1466, the dogs were sniffing around the two bloodied corpses dumped at the port. Only one ship remained at the waterfront.

The third time I entered Father's study legally, through the door, I was accompanied by the solicitor Hermann van Severin, the new nanny and Ondre.

'Rembrandt's *Faust*?' Hermann van Severin exclaimed in reverence.

'Etching,' I said.

He looked at me with approval, although I didn't really know what I was saying. I went over to the desk. Two and a half steps to the left. I bent down and took out the big tube with the red velvet lining. The map of the world upside-down was rolled up just the way I'd left it a few months earlier. The trail of my tongue had gone. I sighed with relief.

'It was the wish of my friend Adolf Alois Adler, your father, that you continue your studies at the Jesuit school, then go on to study medicine and take over his practice. Until you reach adulthood, I will be the guardian of the estate,' explained Van Severin.

We went out to bow our heads at the catafalque where my father's body was resting. No candles had been lit on the ground floor.

'Now you'll be in charge of the servants,' said the guardian of my inheritance, and I understood that for the first time I was responsible for something. But what? I needed instructions. I'd have given anything for someone to tell me what to do.

I curse that moment; I curse and curse again—that moment, and everything that followed. I bury my old, wrinkled face in my bony hands; my shoulders, covered in a monastic cloak, shake with dry sobs. For I know what I must do, what I will do in the future, and I know why it must be done.

In the evening I dismissed Nanny and Ondre and stayed in the house alone. My father lay in the hallway surrounded by flowers. He looked like he always did. Just even less interested in me.

That night I went into his study again. The desktop was illuminated by the moonlight. Standing strong and resolute, I opened the drawer. Its edge came up between my legs. For the first time, I felt the hard resistance of substance there. The pressing of the wooden edge delighted me. Excited, I slid the map of the upside-down world out of the red-velvet-lined tube.

I spread the map out on the desktop. Dry, thin, rustling parchment, almost translucent. I touched it. I stroked it, slipped it back and forth between my fingertips and nails until they bled. Balancing on the balls of my feet, I rubbed against the hard surface, against the edge of the drawer, against everything. I ground, I lashed out, I inflicted pain until the first shiver shook my body. Then came the waves of ebb and flow. With each contraction my sense of guilt dissipated, and a powerful desire to conquer arose within me. I yelled and howled, my wails tearing through the quiet of the port city. The dogs panicked and fled.

Fra Mauro's map disappeared that night.

'I will not rest until I have it in my hands. I will not rest to the end of my days!' Andreas Bianco knelt down on the pier, which was red with blood. He ran his talon-like fingers through his mop of black hair. Illuminated by the moon, his face was twisted in despair.

From the picture, Faust looked at me in horror.

To the distress of my father's friend and guardian of my inheritance Hermann van Severin, I did not become a doctor. At the age of twenty-two, with the encouragement of Father Nathaniel, I joined the order of Societas Iesu.

'I'm counting on you, son,' he said to me one evening as we took our usual walk through the monastery gardens. Small clouds of steam rose from his mouth. It was March 1968, and extremely cold in Hoboken, Antwerp, northern Flanders. 'I'd be proud of you if you were able to take this step. Oh, I don't doubt that you have the courage, but in addition to courage we expect obedience,' said my wise Father Nathaniel, who knew what I needed.

And so after two years of the novitiate and four years of study, I reached my third probation and took a vow of obedience to the Pope. After that, I began working in the Ignatian library. Far from my ambitions and desires, at the Jesuit college in Heidelberg. I was probably sent there because of my Germanic heritage. And my aversion to books.

Working in the library was deathly boring and, at the age of thirty-five, I felt like an old man. The books didn't interest me in the least. I liked the fact that they were neatly categorised and arranged on solid bookcases made especially for them, but they were bulky and heavy. Much like the German nuns I saw every day in the cathedral.

I could request a new posting once every six years. I was counting down the days.

Two months before my *effugium*, as I was gathering books to send to the bookbinder's, suddenly, right above my lowered head, she spoke, in the language only my mother had spoken with me.

'Excuse me, I was sent to you by the abbot, my uncle. Do you speak Polish?'

Do I speak Polish? I looked up.

'Polish, German, Flemish, Italian, Russian...' I was talking nonsense just to stop her from leaving, to keep her there, to keep the jug whole.

She took three books about fifteenth-century history into the reading room. She was interested in torture devices and interrogation methods. She pored over them all day. She went to the toilet twice. I heard her skirt rustling as she walked. I usually closed up at twenty past eight. It was just after eight.

I went very near to her. So near that I could see her pink ear, as thin as parchment, lit from below by the lamplight. I stood and looked at the grey-blue veins in her warm skin. I stooped lower.

'We're closing in fifteen minutes,' I whispered.

I could smell her. It was raining outside.

'Could I take the books overnight?' she asked.

I nodded. I searched for a suitable Polish word for the situation, but all I found was: 'Wait.'

I went out into the corridor with her.

'Wait,' I repeated, and she touched her front teeth with the tip of her tongue but didn't wet her lips. They remained dry.

I got permission to accompany the abbot's niece to her house two streets away. The evening meal started at half past eight with a prayer and a reading. I could have made it, but I didn't. I had my hands full with the books, we didn't talk. The streets were wet. She turned to me in front of her gate, took what I was carrying without a word, and held out her hand to me. A dry, small, weak hand. I could feel her everywhere: in my loins, in my stomach, beneath my ribs and skull. I still remember that weakness after all these years.

That night I tried to remember where I knew her smell from. My body lay on the white sheet in the cell where, apart from the bed, there was only a chair and table. My body. I could see it clearly. Stretched to the limits of possibility, and beyond, a body in which nothing was hidden, dominated by absence.

The map. She smelled of the map. Of dust and light. Of my father's study. That was it.

I buried my face in the pillow and cried for the first time in my life. All night long.

Now that I'm old, when I see that other me, I stretch out my arms to him and I'm choked by an emotion people my age rarely feel. I wish I could tell him that even if he destroyed all the maps of the world, the world would always be there. The worst of all possible worlds. I wish I could—but would it help? It would not. So I just stand there with my arms stretched towards him.

And we spent the night like that—he and I.

He awoke in the morning covered in blood. Giovanni's body lay nearby. The medallion and the secret copy of the map made for the King of Portugal, and paid for with his money, had vanished. Andreas staggered to his feet from the wet pier. The salt water had dried quickly in the Italian sun and every wound on his body burned as if he'd been tortured. He howled and yelped all the way to Giovanni's studio. He had no reason to return to his place. He washed in the bowl of water that Giovanni had used the day before to cool the medallion with the image of Fra Mauro's face.

It was just after midday, the beginning of May, when he returned to the quay.

'Where did they sail off to this morning?' he asked, but the man to whom he directed his question only hawked and spat.

'If I had loose lips, I'd have paid with my life long ago.'

A coin glistened in mid-air, making no sound.

'The same place they're going.' With the stump of his left arm he pointed to a black dhow, a slaver. 'If you pay, they'll take you,' he drawled through his teeth.

Andreas would have paid any price, but in the end he paid very little. He joined the crew of the black vessel that very day.

'I won't rest until I recover the map. Until I find it, death shall not befall me.'

For sixty days I skipped the evening meal. She was in the reading room every day. Every day until 8.20 p.m. After closing, I accompanied her to her gate. We barely spoke at all.

'Where are you from?' she asked once.

'Hoboken, in Antwerp, northern Flanders,' I replied. 'And you?'

'Poland. Bydgoszcz. You won't remember that name, it's too hard,' she said, and then uttered the magic word: 'Bromberg. That's what it used to be called. I'm going back there in three days.'

I died. And she held out her hand to me, then walked away. I descended to hell. I had three days to be resurrected. I asked the prior for a pass to visit my home on an urgent family matter, and I travelled to Hoboken. For one day.

On the day before her trip to the city of Bromberg on the River Brda, Poland, I gave her the black tube lined with red velvet which for centuries had contained the most delicate material, made from the skin of unborn lambs taken from live mothers. On that material, in the fifteenth century, using particles of gold, Andreas Bianco had drawn an exact image of the world conceived in his mind.

At 8.20 p.m. we left the reading room of the Jesuit college in Heidelberg on the River Neckar, Germany. We were silent for the whole walk. I averted my gaze so as not to look at her profile, her movements, her body stirring beneath her dress. Charcoal-grey, almost black.

We went through the gate where we always parted, but this time she didn't offer me her small, dry hand. I remember the weakness of that hand. We entered the building. She led me down a stone staircase to the basement. A low ceiling. The cold, the smell of old stone walls, earth and something else. Darkness. In its final act of desire, the begrudging sun was peeking through a narrow window just beneath the vault, delaying until the last moment its departure into the night. She turned her back to me. The white crescent of her wrist flashed as she undid her dress. And there it lay at her feet—charcoal-grey, almost black. The parchment of her bare back—a map of the whole world. So real that I had to find out whether the trail of my tongue had remained on her. It hadn't. I knew what she wanted from me, but I needed detailed instructions. Had she told me what to do, I'd have been forever in her service. Instead, I was condemned to an eternal absence.

I curse. I curse three times over. I curse the whole world of Fra Mauro, Andreas Bianco, Giovanni Boldù, Faust, Rembrandt, Hermann Stübben, Ondre, Adolf Alois Adler, all the angels and saints. Now and forever. I bury my old, wrinkled face once again in my bony hands; my shoulders, covered in a cardinal's *ferraiolo*, shake with dry sobs. On my knees in the hospital chapel in the Polish city of Bromberg, I curse this world. For I know what I must do, what I'm about to do. There's a plan. I've seen it. I know.

Before she left for Poland, I went to Hoboken for the first time in six years. When I opened Father's drawer to take out the map, it reached to just above my knees. I put both hands on the black desktop and leaned down low. Night. The red roofs, old tenements, the Cathedral of St Martin and St Nicholas, the granaries on the River Brda, the remnants of the Jesuit church. The hospital.

Outside it smelled of wet chestnut flowers. Inside, the scent of Lysol and starched sheets. The clock on the wall. Five past eight. Bed, chair, patient chart. Everything's here.

Date, description, temperature, heart rate, breathing. I read carefully, focusing on the letters so as not to look at her face. I read the chart like a map. She's sleeping.

'Your Eminence,' says a nurse in a blue uniform, 'just fifteen minutes more.'

I raise my head and realise that I'm kneeling by her bed— me, a cardinal. The respirator whirs quietly, the narrow rubber tube pumping oxygen into her lungs. I struggle to my feet. A thin, long, bony body. Jesus, how my body aches, I think. It aches. Twenty past eight. Little by little, an old man, I leave.

At the end of the corridor, straight ahead, is the chapel. It's a good place for people like me. I wrap my cape tighter around me and sink on to the prie-dieu. Your Eminence! I listen to the sounds of the hospital. One by one, they die away. The nurses' footsteps fade. The doctors catch some sleep on fold-out beds. The moon glimmers with the light reflected from the white of the sheets and the parchment of her body.

It's almost four in the morning. On my back, I feel the gasps of the sun as it races, hurrying towards the dawn; but it doesn't get there, plunged into darkness for all eternity, unrequited. I am decoding the characters of history. Medical history.

She's sleeping. I disconnect the oxygen tube from the respirator for three minutes. I count.

And then you open your eyes and look at me for an impossibly long time.

The Butcher's Son

The premiere was to be on the fiftieth anniversary of the October Revolution at the beginning of November. A classmate was busying herself over the set; the stage manager smoked one cigarette after another. The pigeons were crapping on the statue of Adam Mickiewicz. There was always some dreary guy in sunglasses standing outside the theatre. What the hell did he need sunglasses for? Dusk falls before noon in November. On the anniversary of the October Revolution, the sun doesn't rise at all. We were twenty then and we didn't know shit about the world.

The premiere was to take place on the day of the fiftieth anniversary and rehearsals were in full swing. I stood waiting for her outside the theatre, as if by accident, as if I just happened to be passing and I'd be glad to accompany her. The guy in the sunglasses spat, peeled himself away from his section of the wall and followed us. I thought he was following her. I thought it was her.

The term was over, the students were revising; I barely passed because the set designer took up a lot of my time. And then March began, and the strike. You know what we were fighting for? For speech. For freedom of speech. Can you believe that?

The girls at the halls of residence set up a field hospital. They tore up shirts to make bandages and waited all night for the wounded. Apparently, they didn't sleep that night, they just waited. Sensible, beautiful young women. Beautiful. They were truly beautiful. I think, were it not for that set designer, you wouldn't have ended up standing before us in the courtyard that day in March. Were it not for that set designer, I probably wouldn't have been there. You wouldn't have been there either. We wouldn't have been there. Although that was the last time we were together. Wasn't it?

You came out to meet us in a jacket. Not in uniform, just the jacket that usually hung in the hallway. Bottle-green corduroy, the smell of unfiltered Sport cigarettes, the keys to the company car, a Zaporozhets, in your right pocket. When I was little, I broke the heating and it was always on full blast after that.

You came to us in civilian clothing, tall, slim, black hair combed into a wave, the barely discernible shadow of stubble on your cheeks, sharp eyes under thick, dark brows, a smile playing across your narrow lips. It seemed strange to me, how casual and normal you were. I almost believed you. Almost. My male friends admired you. My female friends adored you. You made jokes left, right and centre; I was the first to laugh.

I was the first one they took the next day at dawn. You were standing in the hallway, calm, composed. You didn't say a word. You picked an invisible speck of dirt from my jumper and closed the door behind me. Was that the last time you saw me? I think that was the last time I saw you. Wasn't it?

The first interrogation lasted forty-eight hours. I didn't say a word. I sat on a stool; there was a light bulb hanging at eye level. The operations officer stood at the window. At my side, the enforcement officer. Short, broad-shouldered. His light-brown hair was falling into his eyes. He brushed it away with the back of his hand. There was something boyish in this gesture. There was someone else behind me. I could feel his breath, his smell and his gaze. I sensed his presence the whole time. You weren't there, were you? You don't know who it was?

The enforcement officer knew what he was doing.

That night, after the interrogation, as I lay in my cell, I disintegrated into body and... I was standing beside myself, watching as I lay in my own blood. Something inside me howled, whimpered, cowered from the pain and froze. Someone looked at me through the peephole. You weren't there, were you?

Then I dreamed that I was the son of a butcher.

My mother was the most beautiful woman in the neighbourhood, but Grandfather married her off to Martin Hermanson, a man with a good, solid trade—a butcher. She was satisfied, no doubt. My father was full of vim and vigour and, as he said himself, he knew how to use it. He was not tall, he only reached up to Grandfather's shoulders, but he had a broad chest and was made up entirely of muscle. I had seen him washing in the yard many times. He took off his bloodied apron and shirt and plunged both arms into a bucket up to his shoulders. The blood and water ran down his back and soaked into the black earth in summer, or the white snow in winter. I want to be like him. That's what I want.

I was his eldest son. Thin and frail, but skilful enough to be able to fight my way out of many things. I don't know who I inherited my black hair and dark eyes from. Father's eyes were hazel, his hair short and brown. My parents had seven other children, all of whom resembled my father. I don't count the ones who died, nor the ones who were born after I started working with Father Roderyk.

Up to the age of twelve, I worked with my father in the abattoir that belonged to my grandfather, Franz Saumetzger. With a single thrust of his butcher's knife, Grandfather could slaughter three wild sows at once. Truth be told, Grandfather's knife was a Polish sabre that he'd bought at great expense in 1610, when he was still young. It was a worthwhile purchase. Each time he killed three at once, he would kiss his knife, smear his lips with blood and remind himself that it was worthwhile. I think the butcher's knife was the one thing with which he was truly satisfied.

After Grandfather's death, Father ran the abattoir with just me, which was good, because he could teach me everything, and I could do everything. Even though I was as thin as a rake, I could hang up a buck, skin it and butcher it all by myself. I didn't tear the skin, nor damage the meat. The first time I did it, Father just stood and watched, and later at dinner he said loudly, so that everyone could hear, 'He's destined for greatness, this boy.'

And then, so that no one forgot, he added, 'Don't forget that.'

Mother sold meat in the shop at the front of the house. Once a month we delivered meat to the monastery. When Grandfather Franz was alive, he made the delivery. He'd sometimes take Mother along to help. I understood that she'd been helping him from a young age. Before she got married, she was still taking the meat to the monastery. After Grandfather died, she was the only person who could do it. Father and I were too busy at the abattoir, my brothers were too young. And someone had to do it.

One day, a monk came to us from the monastery wearing a long, hooded cloak. He arrived on a beautiful chestnut horse with a live weight of no less than 100 stone. Pure muscle beneath glistening skin. Skin like that alone was worth all the money in the world.

'Do you like her?' asked the monk, and I lowered my eyes because I wasn't supposed to talk to customers. He wanted to speak to Father, so I took him through to the back and left them alone. When he left, he patted me on the back of the head.

At the dinner table, Father slowly put down his spoon and said, 'I'm sending Mattijn to serve at the monastery.'

Then he said a prayer and began to eat. Mother didn't eat a thing that evening.

In the morning, the monk arrived with a spare horse to take me away. Father put his hand on my shoulder but didn't say a word. That was the last time I saw him.

It was autumn. I was about to turn fourteen.

'What's your name, son?' asked Father Roderyk when I was brought before him. I could only see half of his face. A deep hood covered his forehead, eyebrows and eyes. The shadow of his hooked nose cut across his thin lips, his lower jaw tautening the muscles of sunken cheeks outlined in dark stubble. Waves of dark hair reaching to his shoulders spilled from beneath his hood.

'Mattijn Hermanson, son of Martin the butcher,' I replied.

There was silence in the room. Not a single sound penetrated the thick walls from outside. The shadows in the corners seemed to be whispering prayers I didn't know. For the first time, I could hear the beating of my own heart. Or maybe someone else's?

'What can you do?'

I knew what I could do, but I couldn't say it.

'Give me a pig and I'll show you what I can do.'

The corners of Father Roderyk's narrow mouth twitched and he bowed his head slowly. Then Father Roderyk stood—he was very tall—and said, 'Take him.'

I was taken to the stables, where I was to look after the monastery horses, although I don't know why, because there were two monks there who preferred to do everything themselves. As well as the horses, there were three dairy cows and a fourth in calf. What did they need a butcher's son for? I had nothing to do.

In November it snowed. In the morning someone came into the stable and shook me by the arm.

'Do you know how to kill a cow?'

I just shrugged in response. What kind of question was that?

We went down to the cowshed.

She was young, it was her first calf. She couldn't give birth to it. I could hear from a distance that she was dying. Black, pus-filled blood was running down her legs. I could finish her off, but I had nothing to do it with.

'What can I use?' I asked. The monk gestured to the manure fork. I laughed. 'I've never done it with a fork before.'

I went to the kitchen to get a knife. I chose the biggest one.

'Get Father Roderyk, he wanted to see how it's done.'

We waited for him, the dark cow mooing.

Finally he came in and stood to one side. He buried his hands in his habit. Tall, thin, he looked at her from beneath his monastic hood. He nodded for me to start.

I slit her throat, deep, in a single movement. Father Roderyk took two steps forward. She was still staring with her wet eyes, but she'd stopped breathing. One leg was still kicking. I opened up her abdomen and pulled out the rotten calf. It must have died inside her long ago. Those standing near backed away. One vomited up the contents of his stomach outside.

'Had she been mooing like that for long?' I asked.

No one answered.

I tied a rope around her hind legs; a few men had to help me hang her because I didn't have a pulley. I put out a bucket for the blood. Father Roderyk couldn't tear his eyes away.

'What shall we do with her?'

Again, no one answered. It seemed a shame for her to go to waste, so I sliced into her groin and skinned her while she was still warm. I knew from Grandfather that black skin is more sturdy than white. Then I cut off her head and removed the tongue, the brains and the gullet. While cleaning the stomach, I had to be careful not to dirty the offal so it wouldn't become bitter. The meat was ugly and lean. The cow had been heavy with young and must have been suffering for a long time before being slaughtered. But a job is a job. It took about four hours. Father Roderyk stood watching the whole time. The others had gone, but he stood and watched. His hands were buried in his habit.

I was terribly cold in the stables in winter. One night, Father Roderyk came and woke me.

'Get up and come with me,' he said.

So I got up and followed him.

'Bring your knife.'

A big moon was shining, reflected twice in the motionless sea. We descended the hill from the monastery, walking through the sleeping town towards the port. The black bulks of the ships looked as mighty as huge rocks. At the very end was the *Nuestra Señora*. I was speechless with wonder. Never before had I seen anything so beautiful as the shape of this frigate drawn in silver moonlight against the black sea. The navy-blue sky was drowning in the ship's straight masts and empty yards.

We boarded the ship. Father Roderyk handed a crew member three bags of coins.

A man in a green velvet caftan led us down a steep staircase below deck.

'Poor things, they have no souls. They look like people, but they don't understand human speech, nor do they have feelings. And they don't believe in one almighty God,' he said in a hard accent.

We nodded.

We descended further and further down the steep staircase. It was mercilessly hot. There was nothing to breathe.

At the very bottom, on the lowest level, there were Black men sitting in cages, chained to the bars. Their bodies glistened in the torchlight. The whites of their eyes shimmered.

The man with white shirt cuffs protruding from beneath the folds of his caftan pointed to the left where some bodies were laid out along the ship's side. Two adults and one child.

'They're yours,' he said.

'You're going to skin them,' said Father Roderyk.

'Here?' I asked.

Father Roderyk nodded.

I got to work. I cut off the heads and set them aside.

The man in the green velvet wanted to get some sailors to help me hang up the bodies. There was no need. The ropes on this ship were of the highest quality, the pulleys worked like a dream. If we'd had equipment like that at the abattoir, Father would have been in heaven.

'Shall I cut up the flesh?'

'No. We just want the skins.'

In technical terms, the work wasn't difficult. The bodies were fresh and there was no fat between the skin and the flesh. All it took was a few good incisions and it easily came away from the tissue. It didn't even need much cleaning. But it required strength and precision. The two adults didn't take long. I left the child for last. His skin was much more delicate, I had to be very careful not to damage it. I tried to make incisions that would be invisible, from the knees, up along the inside of his thighs to his anus. It went perfectly.

It was terribly hot and stuffy. My back was aching and sweat was dripping into my eyes. I straightened up, wiped my forehead with the back of my hand and glanced towards the opposite corner, where a large Black man was pressing his face against the bars of his cage. His eyes were fixed on me. His hands were chained behind his back. Snot was dripping from his nose, saliva from his open mouth. His eyes were large and shiny, surrounded by black skin, reminding me of an animal.

'That's his father,' said the man in the velvet caftan.

'Finish up now. It's dawn,' said Father Roderyk dryly.

With great care I laid the child's black skin on the floor. The sailors let down the corpses and put the skins into sacks.

The father was whimpering quietly as we went up on deck.

Outside, a fresh wind was blowing off the sea. The day was breaking.

We were heading south in the spring sun.

The prior had come to us just before we left. He seemed so small and lost in the big monastery courtyard. Father Roderyk knelt down before him, and the prior laid his hands on his head.

'May you be guided by Fra Mauro, the unparalleled cartographer, patron of travellers and those who have lost their way,' he said, and hung a medallion with an image of Fra Mauro around Father Roderyk's neck, his shrivelled profile in a monk's cowl. 'May a safe, straight road lead you to the Holy See.'

Father Roderyk bowed his head and stood. The prior turned and walked away.

'His Holiness is waiting for the exhibits,' said Father Roderyk to the monk who was loading the sack of well-cured skins on to the horse.

Father Roderyk mounted the horse. I set off behind him.

'All roads lead to Rome,' he said, and he didn't speak another word for the entire journey.

He was also observing a strict fast. He didn't drink wine, only beer, and he ate nothing besides dinner. I looked at him with reverence. He was a holy man, and he looked like one.

We travelled a well-trodden path, and people from the villages and towns would bow before us and step back to let us pass. The news that Father Roderyk was on his way to Rome with gifts preceded us and paved the way. Only once was the crowd too big to pass. Faithful Christians asked Father Roderyk for a blessing; in silence, he raised his white hand and made the sign of the cross. Never before had I seen such a throng of people. A guard had to disperse them so that we could get through.

A few days later, we reached a monastery on a hill where they were expecting Father Roderyk. A young lad took our horses from us. Father Roderyk requested a moment of private prayer in the Chapel of the Blessed Virgin. I waited for him at the door. I sat on the steps and ate some bread and dried meat. A monk in a black habit came to show us to the dormitory. Father Roderyk had a cell with a window and a bed. There was a view out on to the Tyrrhenian Sea. A table beneath the window, a Bible on the table, water in a jug. I looked at the book, but I couldn't read. I didn't know the letters. I wasn't interested in them anyway.

There was no window in my cell. I lay on the straw mattress and stared into the darkness. I tried to make out the shapes of the table and chair. Someone walked down the corridor to the outhouse. For a moment, the flickering candlelight seeped in through the gap between the door and the stone floor. Enough for me to see that someone was sitting at the table. I reached for the knife under my mattress, but I wasn't quick enough. I felt a rope around my left foot, a sharp jerk, and I was hanging upside-down. I couldn't see the person who tied me up or the one who held the rope. The blood rushed to my temples. Someone's agile hands were stripping off my clothes. Someone hit me on the head.

I lost consciousness.

I was roused by a torrent of cold water. A light bulb was giving off a weak glow. I was lying naked on the concrete floor.

I looked at the world with one eye. The other I couldn't open. I could see only their shoes and the bottom of their trousers. A telephone was ringing down the hall.

Someone was standing behind the door. I recognised the smell of cigarettes and cologne; I sensed a familiar presence. You must have been there, Dad. You must have known.

Someone kicked me in the stomach. I threw up.

'Leave him be,' said a voice from behind the light.

I lay naked until dawn in a pool of water and puke. It wasn't until the sun was tracing a bright rectangle on the floor that they picked me up and took me to my cell. So help me God, I didn't care what they asked me.

'Name?'

'Albert Einstein, son of Hermann.'

The enforcement officer's fist flew across my face. I spat out blood and mucus.

'Name.'

'Isaac Newton?'

'You son of a bitch.'

A punch to the stomach, I doubled over. A strong pair of hands brought me back up straight.

'Name.'

'Immanuel Kant, son of a whore.'

I must have told them everything they wanted, perhaps even more. If they'd ordered me to admit that I was the son of the devil, I'd have signed the pact in my own blood.

I woke up dog-tired, as if I'd been fighting someone all night. At first light, before matins, we resumed our journey. We rode along the coast. The colour of the Tyrrhenian Sea changed depending on the time of day. At dawn it was green, restless and elusive. At noon it was blue, a blue like I'd never seen before. In the evening it fell into darkness with a shimmering surface. For a brief moment it was black, then it blazed with a million stars.

We were headed for Rome, carrying gifts for His Holiness. We were untouchable.

We entered Civitavecchia before the Sabbath. Father Roderyk took us directly to the Cattedrale di San Francesco, where we were received with great ceremony. Father Roderyk was asked to deliver a sermon. This would surely delay our journey, but the tormented souls of Christians were yearning for the words of truth from Father Roderyk's lips. What was an extra day for the salvation of mortal souls? Father Roderyk assented.

The cathedral was thronging with people. The nobles were sitting on benches, while the poor crowded into the cloisters, the side chapels and under the organ loft. Father Roderyk rose from his slab of stone and ascended to the pulpit. I watched him from the sidelines. He was slightly hunched over, although because of his height he appeared to be standing straight and proud. In complete silence he cast his eyes over the faces of the gathered townspeople. Everyone held their breath under his gaze. One more moment, I thought, and they'll suffocate, but he took a breath and thundered: 'Your city is beautiful and charming. You have fortified gates made of white marble. But what are you guarding, brothers? You have nothing left to guard. You have equipment to fight fires. But why do you need to fight fires in the city? You cannot fight the heresy in your hearts. You have a lighthouse to show the way to those who are lost. But why do you need to find your way at sea? In your spiritual life, you have lost your sense of direction.'

His speech was inspired, his words full of passion. I could see only the black profile of his face against the sharp arc of the window. The crowd swayed, but he calmed the human sea with a single wave of his hand.

'Ravenna, my home town, is a bastion of Christ's only path in the modern world. When I compare this city to yours, I see that we are faithful to our baptism. And you? You allow heretics and sinners to live among you. What has become of your baptism, brothers?' Father paused.

The faithful listened to these harsh words in horror; some of them sensed what was coming but were either unable or unwilling to stop it. For how can you hold back the speeding wind that carries both the ships of grain and the Black Death?

'You are living like guests on your own land. Rid yourselves of the heretics. Return to the bosom of Mother Church. Amen.' Father's chastising hand was still raised in the air.

Nobody moved. Only when the priest brought his hands together and began to intone the Lord's Prayer in a high-pitched voice did the crowd rise.

After Mass I went to find Father Roderyk in the vestry. I helped him remove his robes and wash his hands. He was exhausted. I walked him to his cell. I hesitated at the door. The sack with the gifts for His Holiness was hanging from a hook.

'Do you want to know why we're taking the Black skins to the Holy Father?' I remained silent, despite my curiosity. Father Roderyk continued, 'His Holiness will have them stuffed and displayed in the audience chamber as a warning.'

'Aha.'

'In return, he might allow us to copy a section of Fra Mauro's map, the map that shows the entrance to the first circle of hell.'

'Aha.'

'Do you want to know why sinners go to hell?'

I turned my head to the window. I wasn't interested. The sails of a ship coming into shore loomed on the horizon. Flocks of birds were circling above its masts. The sun glistened on their black wings. I remembered the shining Black face pressed against the bars of the cage. I couldn't breathe. Father was talking about hell.

'Are you listening?'

I was not.

'You can leave.'

I left.

On the calm night waters of the Tyrrhenian Sea sailed Janszoon's polacca, a ship of ill repute, a ship that everyone feared, a ship from the bowels of hell.

We reached Rome the next day. The papal dignitaries sent a retinue to meet us. We entered the gates of the Eternal

City in the proper manner, with a large entourage. I was riding at the rear, keeping an eye on everything.

They accommodated me in a building near the stables, so I saw nothing of Father Roderyk for a whole week. I brushed the horses, sharpened my knife, admired the cathedral, and spoke to no one. The food was excellent, the beer fresh. The fruit was sweet and juicy. I'd never eaten anything like it.

That week, I gathered that Father Roderyk was attending meetings with the Pope to discuss important matters. Perhaps he was briefing him on the situation with Italy's northern frontiers? Or perhaps they were planning how to banish the squalor of heresy from the Church? Or else he was copying that priceless map to discover the location of the entrance to hell.

After seven days, Father Roderyk summoned me to his room. I didn't recognise him; the purple robes had changed him completely.

'We leave tonight,' he said in a dry voice.

He was holding a black tube, four cubits long, sealed with the papal seal at both ends.

'Guard it with your life. His Holiness has entrusted me with Fra Mauro's map. We have three years to study it. This is his gift. We leave this evening.'

I packed the saddlebags and secured the tube to the horse's side, behind Father Roderyk's saddle. We left the Holy See before the sun dipped below the dome of the basilica.

It was still light as we rode out of the Eternal City. We passed the white defensive walls. The road led through the trees, delving deeper and deeper into the forest.

'Let's ride closer to the sea,' I said. 'There the moon will show us the way.'

I didn't dare criticise Father Roderyk for his decision to set off so late.

We branched off to the left. At dawn we would reach the monastery of the Dominican Fathers, who had been awaiting Father Roderyk's arrival following his audience with the Pope. From there, we would be escorted all the way to Genoa.

'The brothers must have sent guards to meet us halfway,' I said, spotting four men on horseback ahead on the road between the line of trees and the sea. In the night, they looked like the horsemen of the apocalypse. Our horses whinnied. Cautiously, we maintained our distance. Father Roderyk drew his hood further over his eyes. The four men reached for their weapons. There was a flash of swords in the moonlight. I realised my mistake. Father Roderyk must have known straight away. Two men charged forward and past us, cutting off our escape route from behind. The two in front obstructed our path.

'I am a servant of Christ. I bring letters from His Holiness Pope Innocent X, governor of God's Kingdom on earth,' began Father Roderyk, but he did not finish.

They dragged us roughly to the ground.

They searched me, their movements expert and efficient. I felt their strong, hard hands all over my body. They took my long butcher's knife from the sheath of my right boot, the knife I had kept with me since that November night in the cowshed.

'What's this?' hissed one man through large, golden teeth, spraying his spit between my eyes. With a single blow, he tossed me to the sandy ground and held his foot against my neck. Meanwhile, two of the men were searching our saddlebags. All they found was a little food, beer, and the black tube sealed at both ends.

'Who are you?' asked the man standing over me. Something in his manner reminded me of the seafarers I used to deal with back home when they came to buy meat. How long ago that was!

'Mattijn Hermanson, son of Martin the butcher,' I replied, and these words seemed almost unreal to me.

'Oh, we've got ourselves a butcher,' he shouted to his comrades. They cackled. They'd just finished searching Father Roderyk and had taken his letters, the bag of coins and the Fra Mauro medallion.

'What is it?' asked one, weighing the medallion in his hand.

'Don't bother asking, you can sell it in some port, Amsterdam or Gdańsk,' snapped the other.

'Come here!' barked the one giving the orders. I clambered to my feet and walked over to him. I spat out the sand from my mouth.

'You're a butcher's son? Show us what you can do.'

The sea crashed rhythmically against the shore. The third-quarter moon shone brightly. The westerly wind snagged in the branches.

'Butcher him.'

Father Roderyk sat leaning against a tree.

'Any one of us would do it with pleasure.' Silence. Nobody laughed. 'But that might be worse.'

He handed me the knife and tore the hood from Father Roderyk's head.

I knelt down beside him. I saw the whole of Father's face for the first time. I looked at his black hair, strong eyebrows and protruding cheekbones. I looked into his face and saw myself. Dark eyes, hook nose, thin lips. He was whispering the words of a prayer I didn't know. I knelt before him, staring into his eyes.

The four men looked at my hands. Their cloaks flapped in the wind.

'Father?' I asked, and he nodded to show he was ready.

I plunged the knife in deep, slicing from his throat to his spine in a single movement. There was a crunch of cartilage and tendons. A spurt of bright, warm blood. I didn't let his head fall, I tilted it back so the blood would flow out. I wiped the knife on his cloak and put it in the sheath.

I'm good at my job.

Father Roderyk stayed there, leaning against the tree. They took me aboard Janszoon's ship.

I spent the night on board. Janszoon didn't even take my knife from me. He didn't even order my hands to be tied. When dawn came, we were on the high seas. A smooth westerly wind was blowing.

They released me at the end of June, without a trace on my file. I had regained my freedom.

I was ecstatic on the road home. My steps on the terrazzo staircase sounded like music. The key in the lock squeaked like a violin. I entered the flat. It was empty. Your jacket wasn't hanging in the hallway. I opened the wardrobe. The wooden clothes hangers rattled. In the bathroom, on the glass shelf beneath the mirror, was the round mark left by the shaving brush. A single towel on the rail.

There was an envelope on the kitchen table. Banknotes inside, but no words. You didn't leave me a letter. No information. No words. I went down to The Wizard for a vodka.

A classmate told me the set designer had fallen in love and someone else was fucking her now. I shrugged. Love is love.

I went to the university on Monday. Classes had finished for the summer. The wooden staircases, empty corridors. The door to the dean's office was open, I went in.

'Record book, please.'

I handed it over.

'Student card.'

The secretary cut it in half with a big pair of tailor's scissors. She did it in a single, competent slice.

'I want to talk to the dean,' I said, not harbouring much hope.

'What for? You're no longer a student at our university.'

I sailed out into the vast oceans of freedom.

I sat by the phone and waited. After all, you might have called to ask: how are you feeling, what are you doing, who are you? And I'd have said nothing for a long time, then hung up. And then you'd have understood that you're no longer my father. That I buried you. That I've forgotten about you. That I don't want to know you. And it would be my decision.

But you didn't call.

A few days after that, I took a trip to Cisna to pick blueberries. I returned three years later. There were no missed-delivery slips in the letter box. No letters from you. Not a word.

So I wrote hundreds of letters to you, thousands of words. After you read them, you'd surely have understood your mistake. Surely. But I didn't send them because I didn't have your address. You wouldn't have understood anyway.

At night I went up on the roof of our block, lay down and looked at the stars, like we did once on holiday in Yugoslavia, after Mum had gone. Remember that sky?

Janszoon's polacca sailed tirelessly north. Janszoon kept his crew under strict control. Each of those thirty men knew his place and his job. At night I lay out on deck and looked at the stars. During the day I scrubbed the deck and bailed out the salt water. I once put out a fire below deck. After that, Janszoon's lads stopped beating me up.

In the summer of 1646 we reached the North Sea. We dropped anchor in July in a fishing village near Amsterdam.

At night, Janszoon disappeared; in the daytime he walked around in a furious mood. He pounded young Jacek when the boy spilled warm grog on his trousers. It was best to stay out of his way.

'You're going with my lads,' he said one day.

We took four horses and set off towards Amsterdam. At sunset we stopped in a forest near Bredevoort.

'We have to reach the port by night. We'll find the *Standvastig* there. It won't be hard, it has three masts,' said Mat, lighting a fire to roast the chicken. 'We just need to lure the captain, Andreas Bianco, ashore.' The damp branches gave off more smoke than fire. 'Fortunately, we have something he wants. I'll give him the tube, he'll give me the money. Then the butcher will slit his throat.' Mat knelt down and blew into the faint flame.

Brand unsaddled the horses. He threw the black tube, fastened at both ends with the papal seal, on to the ground beside me. I knew what was inside. I knew because you told me, Father.

'Be careful with that,' I hissed, plucking the chicken.

'Or what?' Brand leaped towards me, his hand balled into a fist.

'Your future is in there, Brand. Hell is in there.'

Brand's hard fist struck me on the forehead. I could feel the blow inside my skull. The half-plucked chicken slipped from between my knees as I fell slowly on to my right shoulder. Before losing consciousness, I saw a troop of musketeers in the uniform of His Royal Highness emerging from the woods.

The night is overcast. Outside, the wind is battering the boughs of the trees. The windowpane reflects the interior of the room: I'm sitting at the table, looking at the window.

I can see myself. I am hunched and thin. My long grey hair falls in waves over my shoulders. In my black eyes, the sky darkens. I look at my face and I see you.

Faust

The *Standvastig*, indomitable, unyielding and fearless, rocked in the dark waters of the port of Amsterdam. On board, a man was leaning against the railings and staring into the night. Legs splayed wide, fingers gripping the spars, long black hair shining on his temples. He looked like a bird against the night sky.

He was listening out for the hoofbeat of the four horses, but the only sound coming from the shore was the steady beating of the waves against the sides of the moored ships. He waited and waited for the hoofbeat, but nothing came.

It was getting light in the east. Before dawn broke, the man gave the signal to set sail. They left quietly, propelled by oars. Once they had gained some distance, the sails were hoisted.

On the night of 14 July 1646, an almighty explosion tore through the dark of the night. Those who arrived first said there was nothing to be retrieved. The buildings were reduced to ashes. The entire garrison of the fort of Bredevoort was lost, as well as several dozen soldiers and their commander, Sergeant Stoffel Stoffelse, who was known as Jeger on account of his skill as a hunter.

Two days earlier, Stoffelse had cracked down on the cutthroats who had long been harassing travellers on the road from Bredevoort to Amsterdam. Out on an evening reconnaissance with a small troop of musketeers, one of his men had noticed smoke coming from the depths of the forest. They stole up on the ruffians with ease; there were only four of them. They had been plucking a chicken to roast on the fire, but they wouldn't be eating now. The dogs ripped their bodies to shreds. The four horses tied up nearby were claimed for the army. The sergeant's wife cooked the chicken for dinner the next day.

Stoffelse was due to be commended for his actions, but instead he went up in smoke. He left behind his wife, three daughters and three sons—Hermen, Frerick and Berent—one of whom was already a soldier like his father. Stoffelse's widow remarried six months later to a neighbour, Jacob van Dorsten. He turned out to be a good husband and a lenient landlord. He allowed her daughters to remain in the house until spring, so it was not until March that they had to go out into the world.

The eldest was twenty years old when, on a warm, sunny morning, she knocked on the door of a rich painter of whom she had heard tell at the inn. He was rich not because he painted particularly well, but because his wife had left him 40,000 florins in her will to split between him and their son, Titus. And the boy had been looked after since his mother's death by the innkeeper's niece, a woman of around forty, whom in any case the painter—Rembrandt, son of Harmen van Rijn—had promised to marry as soon as he was able to change the stipulation in his wife's will. Unfortunately, her uncle, Hendrick van Uylenburgh, an art dealer and friend of the artist's, had been appointed to uphold the will. The innkeeper himself had told all this to Stoffelse Jeger's daughter, who had taken work at the inn scrubbing the tables and floors.

So, on a sunny morning in March 1647, she stood in the doorway of the painter Rembrandt van Rijn and announced that she could be his housemaid, because she knew how to do everything, she had two younger sisters and three brothers, one of whom was a soldier like her late father, God rest his soul. And first she lowered her eyes and made a face appropriate to the circumstances, then she looked at him and smiled broadly with her red lips, showing her dazzling white teeth, for she saw before her a well-built man with gentle facial features, though his eyes were piercing, and with a shock of hair on his round head. But she was particularly captivated by his nose. It was neither hooked nor snub. A nose like that, she thought, would be the pride of any man. And she stayed with the painter to help out. Not only in the kitchen, but with everything.

He was forty-two years old when, one Wednesday morning, he opened the door—not the front door, but the servants' door. He opened it even though he wasn't expecting anyone, for he was in the habit, when Titus's nanny wasn't around, of opening the door for the beggars and giving them something from the kitchen dresser. So he opened the door and a girl was standing there; she was young and looked hard-working. He hired her on the spot, thinking she would be suitable for the kitchen. For everything, in fact.

The girl moved into the servants' quarters that same day. She brought with her a bundle of linen and a long black tube, sealed at both ends, which her father, Stoffel Jeger Stoffelse, had brought home in the night two days before he died and stowed beneath his daughter's bed. She'd opened her eyes and sat up under her quilt, but he'd said, 'Quiet. Don't tell anyone.'

'What is it?'

'I don't know. But I'll find out when I get back. Go to sleep,' he'd said, and she obeyed.

So when he didn't return from the night watch at the fort of Bredevoort she told no one, not her sisters or mother, not even Van Dorsten, who was letting her stay in the house until spring; she just took her clothes and the tube from under the bed and went to the Amsterdam inn, and now here she was working for the painter.

On Thursday, she woke up in a new place. Balls of fluff under the bed, dust on the windowsill, a wooden trunk long unopened. Empty. She looked out of the window but nothing interesting was happening, so she started cleaning. She wiped away the dust, put her clothes into the trunk. She put the black tube, sealed at both ends, under the straw mattress. Brushing off her skirt, she slipped her feet into a pair of clogs and went to the kitchen to peel carrots.

In the kitchen she bumped into Titus's nanny. It was hard to avoid this old woman, already in her forties, her figure hunched, making her arms look longer and her face bigger, with a protruding chin and receding hairline. This woman whose body was like warm wax, crumpled and increasingly wrinkled beneath her tunic and skirt. The woman who had been waiting for Rembrandt and, as a result of this waiting, had become bitter and was now looking with immense loathing at the new maid who was trying not to get in her way, unsuccessfully.

On Wednesday, a slim young girl in a black, long-sleeved dress entered my second-hand bookshop through the glass door. It was an overcast day, one of those days when the rain turns to snow, and she had no overcoat. I saw her through the window before she came in. Hastily, I put on my jacket—no antiquarian should receive customers without a jacket. But I knew at once that she wasn't a customer. I chased Mandelchen off the table—that cat really does take liberties—and I came through to the front just as she was bending over a magazine.

'Those magazines are from last season, madam, 1937–8,' I said politely in German. '*Was wünschen Sie, bitte?*' I asked, although I'd already guessed what she wanted. Her red lips, dark eyes and raven-black hair braided around her head said far more than words.

It was November and there were many of her sort around. They spoke in a pure High German untainted by foreign influence. They asked for money, food and clothing. Two days later, they went further east and others arrived in their place. Some from Zbąszyń, some from Chojnice. From the border, where it was really bad.

'*Ich brauche jede Arbeit,*' she said.

Suddenly, the sun emerged from behind the clouds and in the blink of an eye her hair seemed fair, so fair. How wonderful it would be if she had fair hair and blue eyes, I thought.

'I can do almost anything, I had younger sisters and a brother, he and my father used to trade in books. I know how to do pricing, for example. I used to help them, before…' She coughed.

The sky became overcast again. That's what happens in November.

'I know these things. I also used to operate my father's bindery in Hamburg, where we lived before the war,' she said, and smiled a smile that made the bookshop grow dark. As if someone had hidden all the books in shadow. As if, suddenly, the light had run out. As if…

She stood in her black dress and stared.

She stood and stared. I know what she was seeing. She saw them, her brother and father, at the *Umschlagplatz*. She saw them. The blackened faces of her sisters. The corpses in the streets, bodies loaded into carts. Acrid smoke under her eyelids. The flies and their larvae. The dogs outside the city walls.

Her lips were red, her eyes black. Hair braided around her head.

It began to sleet outside. Big snowflakes stuck to the window of *Graham Vogel: Alte Bücher*, only to fall in heavy drops a moment later. My neighbour, the widow of a Polish factory owner, was walking along the street. I nodded to her.

'You can sleep in the room upstairs,' I said to the girl.

I took her up. The attic room was dark and empty. There was only a fold-out bed and a wooden chest. Also empty. A dirty roof window which was now covered with wet snow.

The girl laced her fingers together. She had nothing to unpack. I went downstairs. I don't know what she did. Probably went to sleep.

The next morning she was up and ready to work. I made tea and egg on toast. We ate together in the back room. She washed up. I brought out some new acquisitions for cataloguing. I wondered if she could handle this task. I watched her hands out of the corner of my eye. But she worked intently, giving each piece an expert appraisal. She recorded her findings on index cards. Damaged items were put aside. No superfluous movements. She knew what she was doing.

In the evening, she took a tray of hot tea and spiced biscuits to his studio. She rested it on her hip while she made space on the table with her right hand. He watched in silence and let her move the paints and touch the copper etching plates, although none of his students were allowed to do that. Rather than instruct her on where to leave the tea, he stood and watched her precise hand movements, the balance of her hips. The tilt of her body. The light reflected from her white bosom.

When she had left, he reached for some paper and did a quick sketch before her figure faded from his memory. In the background, in the thickets, lecherous, bearded old Jews were lurking, hidden behind the embankment. Should she know about their presence? And should she then resist them, or submit?

He worked long into the night, then went to her room next to the kitchen. He entered without knocking. She was still awake. She was standing in front of the mirror in a nightgown, a comb in her hand. She turned around. With a flick of her hand, she tossed her hair over her shoulder.

He had forgotten that a woman could be a source of such pleasure. Titus's nanny had grown flabby over the years. But this new body was perfectly springy and put up a nice resistance. Every element of this body was clear and smooth, the lips soft, the tongue sweet and moist. Tight inside, but yielding and gloriously warm. He felt that at any moment he would melt into this woman, whose arms and thighs were wrapped around him. But something hard was chafing against his knee. He reached under the mattress, took out a long, black object and threw it to the ground. That moment of distraction had cost him dearly, but happily he felt her hips begin to sway once more. He increased his pace, and she tilted her head back, revealing her broad, white neck. A low, hoarse groan came from deep in his throat. He bit her shoulder, she cried out. He needed her pain. That's what he was waiting for. That's what his body was waiting for. He finished, she was still throbbing. He laid her aside. Her breasts and stomach reflected the cold, white moonlight. He closed his eyes.

In the distance, a single bell was ringing in the church tower.

The bell was ringing from Nieuwezijds Kapel. The rest of the city was immersed in sleep. A great white moon was hanging over Amsterdam.

The lock of hair was moving in time with the breathing of the woman who slept with her head on the thick pillow. Rembrandt carefully slipped from her arms and bent down to look for the shoes he'd been wearing. He fumbled in the dark but found only the left shoe, the right must be under the table. He tried to reach it, but his stomach prevented him. And his back. His lower back had been aching more and more of late. He was working too much on his feet. He bent down with difficulty. The black tube was lying far back, near the wall. He'd thrown it there himself when... There was no sign of his right shoe. Rembrandt reached for the tube, hoping the shoe was behind it. No luck. But he needed both shoes, he had to get out of here, go through the kitchen, down the hall and up the stairs, silently passing the door of the room where Titus and that woman were sleeping, and get to his own bedroom. While pondering a solution to this uncomfortable situation, he examined the tube. To open it, he would have to break the seal. It cracked with a dry pop. He reached inside. He had hardly expected to find his right shoe there, but what he saw truly surprised him. Enveloped in an interior lined with red velvet was a roll of parchment. As gently as he could, he slid it from the soft interior and carefully spread it out on the table.

It was clearly a very old map. The moon illuminated its every detail. Rembrandt immediately appreciated the precision of the drawing, the confidence of the strokes and the immense amount of work involved. He touched the inscription in the upper corner. The swell of the majuscule lettering vibrated beneath his fingers. He leaned his hand on the table and gazed in speechless admiration. Wearing one shoe, the sleeves of his oversized nightshirt rolled up, his nightcap slipping down the back of his head.

In the moonlight, the shadows were cast more densely, and the white shone with a cold, pale-blue glow. The map depicted the shape of yet-unknown seas. Lands, countries and cities that didn't exist. That had not yet come into being. A map of the world that was about to become, that had been presaged and concocted.

In the moonlight, everything began to tremble, move, live. Rembrandt felt someone's hand on his shoulder, he turned around, but the woman was still sleeping soundly, her head on the pillow. He looked at the map again and then… And then he saw it. Clearly. Palpably. He rolled it up hurriedly, stuffed it into the tube and darted out of the room. He wasn't quiet at all. He was terrified.

Rembrandt slammed his bedroom door shut. He tried not to think about what he had seen, but he saw it still, he could still see their faces. Blackened lips, twisted bodies. Some with eyes open, others as if they were sleeping. At first, they were put into coffins and laid in a pile, tens, hundreds.

'I'm cold,' said his woman, her lips turning black. He covered her with a grey woollen blanket.

Those who are doing this will be next, he thought. And he wanted to warn them, to cry out: run away, leave them, they're corpses—but his voice stuck in his throat.

And they went back and forth, carrying, setting down and returning for more and more, and yet more cold, black, heavy bodies. So very many. They stiffened quickly. It was hard to grab hold of them, lift them, move them and drop them. First, they laid the bodies by the walls in a pile. Then they had to dig ditches, pits and tunnels. Within and outside the city. Thousands and thousands.

'I'm cold,' said the woman, her lips turning black. So he kept covering her with the grey woollen blanket. Over and over.

He clenched his fists, dug his fingernails into his skin so as not to see, not to see, not to see. It didn't work. He pretended he didn't know, tried to forget. It didn't work. He knew. He had seen. Children's bodies thrown from windows on to carts full of corpses. Into the streets. Into the courtyards. Naked women, young and old, their eyes and mouths open. Women with black fingers and flabby breasts. Women carrying babies in their bellies, carrying death.

Twisted corpses in the streets. The smoke of burning bodies stung the eyes.

Flies. Swarms of fat flies.

Larvae. Mounds of white larvae.

Dogs. Dogs on the streets of Amsterdam.

Bones. Human bones stripped of their flesh.

He tried to wake up. It didn't work. You can wake from a nightmare, but if you're not dreaming, there's nothing you can do.

'I'm cold,' she said, her lips turning black. And he kept covering her with the grey woollen blanket. Over and over again.

He heard a baby crying behind the wall. He tried not to think. It didn't work.

I told my loyal customers and my neighbour, the widow of the Polish factory owner, that she was my niece who had come from Vienna to study for a year. Nobody believed me—everyone knew that old Graham Vogel didn't have family in Vienna, nor in Berlin, nor in Königsburg, nor anywhere else.

Fortunately, in light of subsequent events, they soon forgot about the girl from the second-hand bookshop on the corner of Holy Ghost Street. And fortunately, she kept a low profile. She knew how to make herself unnoticeable. Around the shop she always wore a black dress with long sleeves, even in summer. She'd be arranging books and suddenly, at the sound of the little bell over the door, she would freeze with her face turned towards the bookcase or bend down, stroking Mandelchen, and no one, not a single person, noticed she was there. Even I forgot about her sometimes.

Since the war started, she'd spent all her time in the back room where there were more and more boxes and crates, because I'd imported several entire libraries at a very low price.

Not only from East Prussia, but also from Wielkopolska and Galicia—that is, from the General Government, Herr Obersturmführer, for the honour of the Third Reich. And from Danzig by sea… *Jawohl, Herr Obersturmführer.*

The largest consignment came from the library of the Lubomirskis in Wiśnicz and Zamość in the autumn of 1942. They ended up in the attic, beneath the window that had long gone uncleaned, next to the empty chest. So she pored over them at night. In the morning, the bells rang at half past six. That's when she went to bed.

As soon as the sky began to grow brighter and more light was seeping into the studio, he set about cleaning the copper plate that was lying in wait by the window. It was so dirty and scratched that it took a few days for him to get it in a half-decent condition. He sprinkled it repeatedly with sand, rubbed it, wiped it, then polished it wet and dry. The whole process would be repeated the following day. Thoroughly and carefully, so as not to damage it. Rembrandt had only a few etching plates, and some of them were also used by his students, rather ineptly. That was why he preferred to get everything ready himself.

This one was almost perfect. He stroked it; as smooth as a woman's skin. His fingers glided lightly over its surface with a pleasant apprehension of fulfilment. But Rembrandt's fingerprints left marks, completely unnecessary, even detrimental prior to the application of the first layer of varnish. He raised the plate to his mouth and breathed out. A dull layer of steam appeared and he wiped at it tenderly in rhythmic, circular strokes until he felt he could move on, then he reached for the warm wax made of resin and greasy soot, which he himself had scraped from the metal elements of the stove to make a silky varnish to apply to the perfectly smooth copper plate. Even, gentle movements, with full awareness that this was only the preparatory stage, that it would still be some time until the first dip of the burin, the use of the needle, the rhythmic deepening of the engravings, to say nothing of the etching. Yes. Before that could happen, he must set it aside. Put it away. Make it wait. Make it yearn. Pretend to know nothing of its presence. It must dry out from longing, set well enough that it was worthy of the hard burin. It must be both resistant and submissive.

Rembrandt placed his prepared material by the window. He didn't even have to make sketches this time. He remembered the whole thing, with the bed and the sleeping woman in the background. Her lock of hair stuck to her forehead. The dark curtains at the windows. Their soft folds. The silhouette of the man bent over the table. His birdlike profile, talons splayed on the tabletop, his face illuminated by the radiance of the map. He already knew every move he would make, every pull of the burin, every dip of the needle. Every groove, every line, every detail. He could see this etching. He knew it. He remembered.

And yet, he felt a desire to look once again at that map hidden in the red velvet interior. To plunge his hand inside, feel the parchment, take it out, spread it on the table, and God! He wanted it. To be immersed in the future, even if it was impossible. Most terrifying.

His body was seized with lust and terror.

He opened the kitchen door.

She was standing by the fire clarifying butter. All illuminated by the red tongues of the flames. Her body smelled of something that reminded him of his childhood. Or puberty, perhaps? She smelled of butter, wax, resin and fire. He laid her on the table, plunged into her warm interior, felt the parchment of her skin. And he looked down at her face.

This was stronger than him. He couldn't escape it. But he already knew.

There would be trouble ahead.

Rembrandt returned to work. There would be trouble ahead.

He worked for a long time. He made the first engravings in broad, slow strokes, holding the burin almost vertically.

Titus's nanny, a woman in her forties, tired and embittered from waiting, kept asking, more and more frequently: 'when'. And since he was still bound by the stipulation of his wife's will—her uncle Hendrick van Uylenburgh, an art dealer, had excellent contacts all over Europe because he'd grown up in Kraków, spent his youth in Gdańsk, then studied in France and Italy—he was unable to marry her.

Rembrandt didn't have time to listen to her. He was working on Faust leaning over the map. High-precision work. He made each stroke rhythmically and sharply: it might have seemed chaotic, but it was not.

There was nothing he could do for her. She was demanding he get rid of the new maid, who had become his lover, so he could stop pretending she was just posing for pictures, because she was well aware of what was going on. After all, she remembered how it was. Did he remember too? That she'd devoted her best years to him, her youth and beauty, she had looked after another woman's son rather than bear her own children. In doing so, she had really risked a lot, even putting eternal life at stake, because she could be excommunicated for what she had done with him.

His burin slipped; he would have to start that stroke again. From the words: 'Do you remember too? Do you remember?'

But Rembrandt couldn't get rid of the young maid with her smooth skin and white bosom. Her body and her tongue. Rembrandt's movements became violent now. That maid who was at once resistant and submissive. The burin lost contact with the varnish again and again, so he reached for the needle; its dry tip and durable shaft guaranteed precision.

Just one hour earlier, Titus's nanny had flung his right shoe down at his feet. 'Here!' she'd said, her face fierce. So there would certainly be trouble ahead, for there were witnesses. The widely respected innkeeper, who was the woman's uncle, and her brother, a seafarer, would both be defending her in court against the painter who had destroyed her life. There would certainly be trouble ahead.

Rembrandt submerged the plate in an acid solution and waited. Then he removed it. He covered some parts in varnish. Others he left exposed. He liked this kind of partial etching. It always gave the desired effect.

He held the plate up to the light and examined it. Next, he wiped away the excess varnish as gently as he could. He cleaned his tools. With his fingers he checked every crevice, scratch and groove. He made sure they were ready and only then began to rub.

There was some paper on the table, thick and slightly damp. She must be deluded. Her demands were preposterous. Just one more smooth thrust. He had to wait for all the paint to run off and infiltrate the fleshy paper. Get rid of the one who gave him pleasure! Preposterous.

He added the date and his initials. He knew what would appeal to Hendrick van Uylenburgh.

It was still quite early, but the city was plunged into darkness beneath the heavy clouds. It was drizzling persistently.

Rembrandt stepped into a brightly lit hallway. A servant took his wet overcoat. There were other garments on the coat stand—Hendrick already had company.

The Eighty Years' War had just ended, and shipping had started up in all directions. There were discussions about transporting grain from Galicia and the supply of colonial goods from Venice. Hendrick's drawing room had been full of people for weeks. There was a constant flow of soldiers, monks, sailors, merchants and Jews in and out.

Rembrandt couldn't have chosen a better time. Hendrick was sitting at a small table with Andreas Bianco, a Venetian sailor and art collector, Father Dominic of Clairvaux, an Inquisitor acting on behalf of His Holiness Pope Innocent X, and Johannes de Renialme, an influential art dealer.

At Hendrick's invitation, Rembrandt joined them at the table. They spoke of the weather and of the English, who couldn't sail for the life of them. And of the beautiful *Standvastig*, the indomitable, unyielding and fearless ship aboard which Andreas had the fortune of arriving into Amsterdam. And of the port of Gdańsk, where a ship loaded to the brim with grain was waiting for a signal. And of the fact that Andreas would be in Poland. And what a shame Hendrick couldn't go. He could do some good business there. And what's the latest with you, Rembrandt? Rembrandt took out *Faust* and set it on the table. Outside, the rain clouds had completely smothered the daylight. The servant turned up the flame in the lamp. The etching shone even more brightly. The map in front of Faust's face.

Dominic of Clairvaux bent low over the etching, but immediately pulled back. He was sure he had seen France in flames. No, it was just the quivering candlelight. But he couldn't take his eyes off Rembrandt's work. He stared at it as if he could see the burning barricades, the cathedral on fire. Was it a coincidence? Could it be a coincidence?

Andreas stretched out his hand. But Hendrick anticipated his move.

'I'll take it! For Staś Lubomirski. I owe him a debt of gratitude, and, as it happens, Lubomirski was just awarded the title of Prince of the Holy Roman Empire by Emperor Ferdinand. The perfect occasion! I'll give him this, Rembrandt, if I may.'

Rembrandt agreed, because he was well aware how much it cost to run his household. And anyway, he was certain there was trouble ahead. That was what he'd come to discuss, but he hadn't had the opportunity.

Andreas was examining the etching carefully. He wasn't the only one.

'How do you know Fra Mauro's map?' he asked, but just then Dominic of Clairvaux began to talk loudly and at length about the ills of Christianity. A very topical subject, and a painful one.

Andreas leaned towards Hendrick. The black hair on his temples glistened in the candlelight like a raven's wing.

'I'll give it to Lubomirski, if you like,' he whispered, 'when I'm in Kraków.'

'Before you go to Kraków, Staś will be visiting me here on his way to Antwerp,' Hendrick replied with a smile, and patted Andreas on the back.

Andreas furrowed his dark eyebrows above his crooked nose, giving him a somewhat predatory look.

Rembrandt started talking to Johannes de Renialme. Both were interested in specific objects that were luxurious and hard to obtain.

Dominic of Clairvaux left first. A few hours later, Andreas bid them good evening, although there was still wine on the table and the conversation had been pleasant. By the time Rembrandt left Hendrick's house, it was completely dark. At that time, the city was almost empty. His footsteps echoed along the dark, empty streets of Amsterdam.

A man shrouded in a long, navy-blue cloak followed him all the way home. When Rembrandt went inside, the man stood at the gate for a long time.

Meanwhile, Johannes de Renialme was questioning Hendrick about Rembrandt. He had plans for him. The impression the inconspicuous artist had made on both the priest and the traveller had not escaped him. Those mysterious curtains and the map, and such an original approach, casting light from that side. The men talked long into the night.

Dominic was also awake. He prayed fervently all night, and in the morning he sang louder than everyone else at lauds: *Deus, in adiutorium meum intende, Domine, ad adiuvandum me festina.* What he had seen the previous evening had filled him with hope. 'O God, come to my aid.' And terror. 'O Lord, make haste to help me.'

Andreas boarded the ship again well after midnight. He didn't speak a word to anyone. He didn't even take off his navy-blue cloak, but sat at the table until morning running his fingers through his mop of black hair. Something was troubling him.

One Friday night in March, she came down the stairs, a lit candle in her hand. Her hand and face emerged first from the gloom, then the dark folds of her dress. I could hardly believe a woman could be so pale.

'It's Rembrandt,' she whispered.

She put a piece of thick paper covered with black printing ink on the table.

'It's Rembrandt's etching. I found it under the cover of the Lubomirski cook…' she took a shallow, wheezing breath, '…book. There's a date and signature.'

Her lips were crimson.

'I know what I'm talking about,' she continued in a frantic whisper. 'My father's friend...' inhale, '...was absolutely crazy about...' exhale, '...his engravings.'

The man in the etching was standing in front of a window, the curtains drawn, leaning with his hands splayed on a table where a map was laid out. All the light was coming from the map. It illuminated his birdlike head, tufts of black hair and sharp features, his piercing gaze fixed doggedly on the drawing of an upside-down world, a world that doesn't exist. That has no right to exist. A world condemned to extinction.

'*Faust*. The non-existent version of *Faust*.'

Her forehead was red-hot and covered in beads of sweat.

'Go back to bed,' I said.

'It's an original Rem...'

'You have to lie down.'

'Look, he moved,' she said, slumping to the floor.

It was 1943, it must have been '43 already, March '43. On the table was a print made 300 years ago, showing Faust bending over a detail in a map portrayed with amazing precision by means of a tangle of lines and strokes carved by the hands of a master. A map that emitted light.

All the rest sank into darkness.

At the end of 1944 it was bitterly cold. For several weeks I'd been burning newspapers and ephemera to heat the tiny box room. More and more often I was reaching for books. I removed the covers, because they didn't burn well, they smoked and didn't give off much heat. Throughout the winter I took books to the widow of the Polish factory owner to burn as well. Once, she gave me two helpings of potato soup in a blue jug. 'Why two?' I asked. Another time, she gave me barley soup. One afternoon in December, along with a six-volume general-history series, I gave her Mandelchen the cat. And that was the last time I visited that old lady, the widow of the Polish factory owner.

Every day at three o'clock in the afternoon, I climbed the stairs to the attic. There she sat in her black dress. She was sorting through the books. I brought her hot tea, soup and bread. Every day.

'It'll all end soon,' I said one day, 'and you'll be able to go back to Hamburg.'

She said nothing.

'You'll be able to go wherever you like,' I repeated.

She looked at me doubtfully, which made me question the truth of what I was saying too. I left the food and went down to the shop.

In January, I packed my things and bought a ticket for the *Gustloff*. It was moored at the port. Its iron sides stood firm against the waves coming off the bay. It was imposing.

On Tuesday I went to take a look at it. When I got home, she was sitting downstairs. She hadn't been down there for twenty months, not since that night she'd discovered the Rembrandt. Her hands were clasped in front of her black dress.

'All the Germans are evacuating. Before the Red Army gets here. I'll find you after the war. In Hamburg or...' I couldn't go on.

She laid a cookbook with darkened pages on the table. From the Lubomirski collection. A question in her eyes. I nodded. I knew what was there. I knew what she'd put between the pages.

We sat facing each other and looked into each other's eyes. In a way, I loved her. Her hands were frightfully cold, her body bony.

The next day, 30 January 1945, we embraced outside the bookshop. I picked up my two suitcases and set off towards the port.

The five captains had been studying the navigation charts, but we still set sail with a delay. I stood among the crowd on the upper deck. The *Gustloff* had 10,000 people on board. Ten thousand. Just after midnight, three torpedoes ripped into its side. I was standing on the upper deck at the time. I was standing on deck.

Darkness closed in around us.

As soon as it was a little warmer, she wrapped up the cookbook from the Lubomirski collection, secured it with string, closed up the bookshop and started walking. Everyone was taking the road to the left, so she went that way too. At first, before they reached the outskirts of the city, it seemed to her that everyone was going around in circles, and so was she. As if she had lost her way and would soon be standing again outside the bookshop on Holy Ghost Street, just like six years ago. But after a few hours of walking, she realised the crowd knew what they were doing. And she followed the crowd.

Some were heading west, others east. For four days she pushed her way against a tide of people moving in the opposite direction, towards Danzig. 'Why are you people going there?' she asked in her head, and answered herself by shrugging her shoulders in her black dress.

How many roads, how many days? Somewhere around Bydgoszcz she was joined by a civilian, tall and straight-backed. From Flanders, he said in German.

'I'm Polish,' she lied.

'Polish women are beautiful,' he said and smiled.

They walked on together. They were going towards Hamburg. In Esterwegen they were stopped by a French soldier.

'I'm a doctor and she's with me,' said the civilian, putting his arm around her shoulders.

Her Polish passport from 1938 opened many roads for them now.

The soldier asked for their destination.

'Hoboken in northern Flanders, Antwerp region.'

The soldier nodded.

They spent that night together in the small town of Meppen, in a boarding house run by two sisters, spinsters. They slept in a small room with one bed. His name was Adolf Alois Adler and he was a doctor, like his father and grandfather before him.

In the morning they continued walking.

They reached Hoboken in northern Flanders on 2 May. The woman whose passport had allowed him to safely cross all borders carried with her a Lubomirski cookbook and an etching by Rembrandt, an undiscovered *Faust* from 1648. Not the *Faust* of 1652, with a nose that was distinctive but not too big, the kind that any man might have, but an earlier one with sharp features and a gaze like the lash of a whip. Not the one looking to the left through the window, but the one reading a map. The one who knows the future.

Adolf Alois Adler hung the *Faust* in his study, consolidating its position.

'You'll give me a son,' he said when it became clear she was carrying his child, whose grandfather Alois Jasper Adler and great-grandfather Jasper Adolf Adler, and whose father, Adolf Alois Adler, were doctors and came from Germania.

In spring, a new farmhand joined the team of servants. He had arrived in Hoboken out of the blue. He didn't seem to know how to read or write, but he was agile and strong. His wind-whipped, saltwater-creased face, the cracked, rough skin of his hands and strong, muscular arms brought to mind seafarers, sailors and galley slaves. He was standing in the doorway, wearing an overcoat, holding an elongated suitcase. The man of the house had just sat down to dinner, but at the sight of the man at the door he jumped up from the table.

'Ondre! What wind blows you here?'

And he immediately took him upstairs to the study.

The dinner had long since gone cold, the child had been put to bed and his mother was bending over her needlework when Adolf Alois Adler came back downstairs with his guest.

'This is our new employee,' he announced. 'He'll be tending to the garden, won't you, Ondre?'

Ondre nodded without taking his eyes off the lady of the house. She looked up at him and thought that she saw in him someone she had seen once, a long time ago.

She must have been mistaken.

At dawn, the world awoke to the screeches of black gulls. Water was pounding rhythmically against the *Standvastig*'s sides. Andreas was no longer on board.

Rembrandt was sleeping restlessly. When he awoke, someone was in his room. The man stood at the window and waited. He was wearing leather gloves. His navy-blue cloak was slung casually over the back of the chair.

'Do you recognise me?'

Rembrandt pushed himself up on to his elbows.

'Let me get up.'

Andreas turned towards the window. It was getting light outside. The first shopkeepers were opening up. Maids with baskets were setting out to fetch the shopping. The cobbled street was coming to life.

'Beautiful etching.'

'It's sold. The next one will be better.'

'I don't want to buy it.'

'No?'

'I want to destroy it.'

'Ah, yes.'

'It's unfortunate that the monk saw it.' Andreas looked around the room.

'Where is it?'

'By the window,' said Rembrandt, pointing. Andreas reached for the etching. He turned it over in his hands for a moment.

'Don't play games. That's not what I'm asking about.'

'No?'

'Where is the map?'

'What map?'

'That one.' Andreas pointed a crooked finger at the patch of light in the etching. Rembrandt shrugged. He tied his trousers at the waist. His fingers were stiff.

'I saw it once. With some sailors at the port.' He was struggling with the knot.

'Once?' Andreas's voice was cold.

'Yes. It's embedded in my memory. Truly impressive.'

Andreas nodded. It truly was. Low clouds were racing over the city.

'The sailors. Who were they?'

'From the east. It was springtime.'

'You're lying.'

'Maybe it was summer?'

Andreas punched him in the face. A flock of birds took flight from the tree outside the window.

'Where did you see it?'

'I don't remember.'

Blood was dripping from his cracked lip. Andreas had thrown a decent punch. Rembrandt put the back of his hand up to his mouth.

'In the port. In July.'

'That's better. The ship's name?'

This wasn't his first time using his fists. He'd made sure it would hurt.

'I don't remember. God!'

Andreas grabbed hold of his arm. Rembrandt's left wrist began to burn, but Andreas kept his fingers tightly clenched around it.

'The captain's name.'

'Let go.'

He didn't let go.

'Don't you value your left hand?' he hissed through his teeth. Rembrandt twisted his body to the left and fell to his knees.

'Janszoon's polacca. They were Janszoon's people. Let go!' he wailed.

A polacca? A renegade ship? Rembrandt was lying on the floor, howling in pain. A ship belonging to Janszoon? Even better!

'You do business with people like that?' Andreas's eyebrows shot up.

Rembrandt curled up on the floor.

Andreas poured acid over *Faust*. The copper plate hissed, then everything went quiet.

'I've been searching for it… I've been searching for that map my whole life. I took my eyes off it one night. I'm dying to know how it got into the hands of Janszoon's people. If you're telling the truth, you can forget about the map. If you're lying,' Andreas bent down low over Rembrandt, 'if you're lying, you'll be beset with misfortune from this day on. By the time you die, you'll have lost everything. Everything. Everything you love. Everyone who loves you. I guarantee it. You will watch their deaths. In the houses, on the streets, in camps and ghettoes. In hospitals, shelters and cells. In cities and forests, in holes and pits. They will die every kind of death. You can't even imagine. If you have lied. I curse your world, curse it again and again.'

Faust sputtered one last time.

Andreas swung his cape over his shoulders. The door slammed behind him.

Ondre dressed plainly, he had long legs and he loved his riding boots. His elbows pinned to his sides, the pit of his stomach tight, he refrained from making any unnecessary movements. His hands were always freezing, so he wore leather gloves, even in early autumn when it was still relatively warm.

She watched him closely. When he didn't know she was looking. He looked like the officer she had seen at the *Umschlagplatz*. He looked like the officer she'd been hiding from all these years.

The new farmhand was staying in the outhouse, but whenever he could, he materialised near her and followed her with his piercing gaze. Sometimes she got the feeling that he wanted something from her. But when she caught his eye, he simply smiled broadly and set about his tasks. What wind had brought him here? And where from?

His name was Ondre. He was agile and strong.

The painter was of no interest to the Holy Office, but his mistress, six months pregnant, was summoned before the episcopal tribunal, which had been convened in response to an act of *publicum malum* perpetrated in the home of Rembrandt van Rijn, a widower of twelve years. Her condition was evidence enough. The trial was short but costly. Rembrandt was afraid that the Church authorities would not only excommunicate the mother but also refuse to baptise the child, and this the painter could not afford. Unfortunately, in this matter, for obvious reasons, he could not count on the intercession of Hendrick van Uylenburgh, uncle of his deceased wife. In this matter he could count on no one.

Unexpectedly, after the third questioning before the tribunal, when the chance of a lenient sentence had reduced to zero along with Rembrandt's funds, and he was also being harassed from the other side by Titus's former nanny, who had finally been locked up in an asylum—just then, an unexpected visitor arrived at his doorstep. It was Dominic of Clairvaux, the monk from the Holy Inquisition whom Rembrandt had met in circumstances that now seemed like a distant memory.

He came inside, looked around and sat down. There was no one in the house to make the coffee.

For a long time, the men remained silent, then at the same moment they took a breath and began to speak: 'Well, good to see you, master.'

'What brings you here, brother?'

And they broke out in nervous, slightly forced laughter.

'You first.' Rembrandt stretched out a hand in invitation.

'I heard about the trial.' The monk shifted in his seat.

'Is all of Amsterdam talking about it already?'

'Not Amsterdam. Our friend Hendrick.'

'Your friend.'

'And he wishes you well, believe me.'

'I have no other option.'

'I'm able to influence the Holy Office's ruling. Because of my position and my long-standing acquaintance with His Holiness, I am able, I could, perhaps… although it's a *negotium impossibilium*…'

'Speak!'

'Do you remember that…' Dominic stroked an imaginary shape in the air, as if it were lying on the table in front of him, as if it were lying there.

'*Faust*? I destroyed it. I can make you another one if you like?'

'No. It's not that. He was looking at…'

Their eyes met, then Rembrandt stood and brought the black tube lined with red velvet from the woman's room. He set it down on the table in front of Dominic in his white habit, who took it from the tube, his hands trembling, for this was the first time he had touched it, and spread it out on the table, real, tangible, and he looked at it for a long time, until he felt that he couldn't look any longer in the presence of this old man, so he rolled it up, slid it carefully back into the tube, closed it, and took it with him.

As he had promised, a few weeks later the Holy Office issued its ruling.

On the last day of October, Rembrandt's daughter was baptised at the Oude Kerk. But her mother—the woman who had once stood at his door and said she could do anything—she couldn't be saved. She didn't have to die, though. She was expelled from the Church. Excommunicated. It's what she deserved for the sin of adultery. Without a doubt. What she deserved.

A strong wind had been blowing for several days. Adolf Alois Adler's wife was returning from church one Sunday, her black dress billowing. She was walking up the garden path when, all of a sudden, Ondre was standing before her.

'I served under your husband,' he said.

They stood facing each other. The wind tugged at her hair.

'Herr Adler was a good commander,' he said. 'He wasn't afraid to give orders. It was an honour to be with him in Bromberg and Danzig. In Königsberg, Kaunas, Vilnius, Riga and Pskov. We were there together,' he said, spreading his arms wide. A heavy medallion lay against his chest. His grey-blue overcoat was flapping in the wind.

The wind tore a bough from a 300-year-old hornbeam. The branch fell near their feet with a dull clatter. The woman went into the house without saying a word.

The *Santa Maria* and the *Nuestra Señora* were waiting to enter the port of Amsterdam. They rolled on the dark waters of the North Sea as if they were cradles being rocked by two nannies, not Spanish cargo ships. It was still a long time until dawn; only then, with the first rays of the sun, could the two vessels safely sail into the harbour. The water's surface, as black as varnish, rippled and foamed. Just before the first glimmers of light appeared on the horizon, the birds rent the air over Amsterdam. Their cry should have awoken the fathers of the city, but they were sound asleep in the arms of their women. An icy wind was blowing off the sea. The *Santa Maria*'s sails shuddered. The *Nuestra Señora* remained unmoved. Both were waiting to enter the port.

In addition to crates filled with black cotton, the *Nuestra Señora* was concealing a dangerous cargo below deck. The glistening, Black bodies of slaves. Their motionless faces, eyes fixed on one point. A few corpses that had not yet been thrown into the water. Rats were scuttling over them, nibbling at their fingernails.

The first hour of dawn enveloped the port in a pink veil. The *Santa Maria* lowered its sails and gangway, and the *Nuestra Señora* followed suit.

The figures of the men going ashore cast long, blue-tinged shadows. It was extremely cold. The Spaniards rubbed their hands together. They would be there for four days. Four days was usually long enough to do the legal trade. Three nights would have to suffice to sell the rest.

The two ships stood side by side with the *Standvastig*. The dark water struck their hulls fitfully, as if it couldn't decide whether to love them or engulf them.

At dawn, one man disembarked from the *Standvastig*.

'You lied to me. It wasn't at the port.'

Andreas stood bolt upright in his leather boots. His raven-black hair was speckled with grey. Time had sharpened his features.

'Janszoon's people haven't seen it. None of them.'

'I don't have it.'

The leather-gloved hand came down on the table.

'I don't have it.' The old man covered his face. 'I gave it away.'

'To whom?'

'Dominic of Clairvaux.'

Titus heard his father cry out. He reached the studio just as the man in the navy-blue cloak was leaving. Their eyes met.

'You'll lose everything you ever loved.'

The *Standvastig* had long since left the port when the *Santa Maria* set sail three days later. The *Nuestra Señora* left Amsterdam the following day. The birds' black wings waved them goodbye. The streets around the port were swarming with rats.

The wind was blowing off the sea, permeating further inland along the canals. It aired the bedding hanging in the open windows, the laundry drying on the lines. It circulated. It swirled. It penetrated. Through and through.

On Monday, Adrian Adler, the son, reached for the milk on the dresser and knocked over the blue jug his mother had brought from Danzig. The jug broke in such an unfortunate way that it couldn't be put back together, there would always be something missing.

That same morning, Adrian's mother went up to the attic, where no one ever went, and opened the window that no one ever opened. She was standing at that window in her black, long-sleeved dress when the wind tossed her to the ground. Everyone was crying their eyes out and Adrian thought it was because of the jug. He was seven years old.

Rembrandt knelt beside her bed. On the other side of the wall, the little girl was crying, the daughter she had borne him a few years earlier, for which she had been justly excommunicated. He had been living under the same roof as a harlot who was now—

'I'm cold,' she whispered. Her lips were turning black.

He covered her with a grey woollen blanket.

There were dead bodies on the streets. Children, women and thin old men. Clothed and naked. Swarms of black flies hovered over them. Dead rats floated in the canals. Dogs were gnawing at bones outside the city walls. Dead bodies everywhere.

At first, they were put into coffins and laid in a pile by the walls of Amsterdam, but it soon became pointless. Those who buried them died first, so their bodies were just thrown into pits and ditches. The city authorities issued an order for corpses to be burned, hoping the Black Death would depart with the smoke. But it didn't.

It was dark in the room. Rembrandt closed the curtains and turned off the light. He looked at her. She looked like she was sleeping. He covered her body and face with a blanket. He knelt beside her bed for a long time and tried to pray, to no avail.

Suddenly he wanted to see it again, reach into the velvet interior, spread the parchment on the table and... God! God!

The Tomb

The quivering torchlight illuminated segments of the stone wall. The man in black cowhide boots moved along the wall with confidence and speed as if he knew the place, as if he'd spent his whole life there. In his tattered overcoat tied with a wide belt, the buckle inscribed with the phrase *Gott mit uns* in gothic lettering, he looked like a monk.

At the end of the corridor was a low door leading to the former library. Its ceiling had collapsed centuries ago, and now the room looked out on to the open sky. Over time, the carved letters over the door had been eroded. *Si Deus pro nobis, quis contra nos?* The man pushed the door open. The heavy hinges groaned. A bird flew out from under the remains of the ceiling and escaped into the night with a screech. The man turned off the torch. In the moonlight everything was as clear as day. The bookcases were located in the stone alcoves. Someone had diligently removed their contents many years ago. Now they were empty and damp.

He walked over to the lectern, which must have had a bookrest on it centuries ago. He knelt down. The old floorboards creaked. He brushed a layer of dust aside. Then he smoothed and stroked, used his fingernail to pry up protruding edges. He was bent over in concentration. How long would this strange prayer take? The moon edged along behind his back, and the sky was brightening in the east when he heaved a sigh of relief and lifted the lid hidden in the podium. Beneath the lid was an opening big enough for a small coffin. The man bent down and plunged his arms in elbow-deep. But he didn't bring out a coffin. He brought out a slim black tube bearing papal seals.

In the morning, the man in the black cowhide boots bought a ticket from Bolzano to Halle in Germany. He carried an elongated suitcase and his overcoat was slung over his left arm. With a spring in his step, he boarded the train.

It was the end of March 1946. Many like him were coming home.

Andrel Weissmann remained on his knees late into the night, leaning against the seventeenth-century carved priedieu in the San Giovanni Chapel in the Dominican church in Bolzano, northern Italy. The verger knew of his habit and allowed him to leave through the back door on the vestry side after the church was closed. The old man always left him a few euros to thank him for the favour.

He was very old now, and each time, he said this would be his last trip to Italy, but he always booked a flight around his birthday in March, during the low season, and returned to old Europe. It was a relief to get out of California. A pleasure to immerse himself in the weak sun, the shade of the narrow Italian streets, the chill of the medieval church.

He always went to the cemetery. He walked slowly, although he didn't need a walking stick like others his age. He unbuttoned his overcoat, clasped his hands behind his back and stopped here and there. He read the plaques, working out how old the dead would have been if they were alive. He didn't lay flowers at any of the graves, but he covered the costs of another year for the tomb of Ondre Bianco, who had been found dead in the Dominican church just after the war. He had died while praying, leaning against the seventeenth-century prie-dieu, staring at Giotto's frescoes.

The curate in the office asked whether Ondre Bianco was family, but Andrel Weissmann shook his head.

'An old friend,' he replied succinctly, holding out an extra 100-euro note in his strong hand.

And now he was kneeling again in the San Giovanni Chapel and staring at the breathtaking frescoes, the crimson, turquoise and purple robes of the damned, their pale faces, big eyes and parted lips. The horses speeding blindly towards perdition. He knelt in front of the wall and prayed not for the salvation of his soul, but to be given the same as them, the damned, to find once again the eternally burning gates of hell. Not the heavenly gardens, nor the hills of purgatory, but the entrance to hell. The never-fading, fiery, bloody walls of the fresco.

As he put the banknote into his drawer, the curate wondered: who was Andrel Weissmann, and who was his friend, Ondre Bianco? But he stopped thinking about them as soon as he closed up the office.

One of them was a clerk. He was in charge of bookkeeping for the fur farms in Trawniki and he was good at his job. He knew that working in a camp was nothing to be proud of, he was aware of what he could write on the form and what he should keep quiet, but it never crossed his mind to change his name. Why should he? He had nothing on his conscience that required a change of identity. He hadn't killed anyone, nor given any orders to kill. He didn't even have the authority to do that! Should he ever be made to confess his whole life's sins, he would have to admit that the one person he might have hurt was the younger sister of Joachim Himlel, his childhood friend. In other words, no one.

So when he arrived in Bolzano in the early spring of 1946 and presented himself at the emigration office, situated in a small room crammed from floor to ceiling with grey files, he was surprised to be told he needed two witnesses to confirm his identity. Why? After all, he'd written clearly on the form in indelible pencil that his name was Andrel Weissmann, son of Klaus, an arithmetic teacher at a German secondary school, that he had been born on 7 March 1917 in Halle and baptised there on 13 May that same year in a Roman Catholic service at the Church of St Nicholas. Since passing his final school exams, he had been working as a bookkeeper. Working for the Third Reich of course, who else? Destination: America. He had no documents with him. No one had documents. Who had documents these days!

Behind him was a crowd of people like him, with no name and no past, who had to leave Europe for various reasons. The glum official didn't have time to focus on Weissmann any longer. The next applicant, his voice full of shame, began to say who he was and to detail his plans for the future. Andrel squeezed through the crowd of representatives of all states and countries, including some who were stateless. In the long, dark, windowless corridor filled with the bodies of foreigners he suddenly felt trapped. His insides were burning.

'Where's the toilet?' he asked in German.

A man with sunken cheeks covered in three days of stubble pointed to a low door under the stairs.

The toilet looked like a torture chamber, but the sharp pain in the pit of his stomach didn't allow him to dwell on it. He unbuttoned his trousers and squatted down. Strips of Italian newspaper for wiping hung from a nail on the wall.

He emerged from the dark stairwell straight on to a street flooded with light. The sun blinded him. He had to blink a few times and shade his eyes with his hand to look right and left. It didn't matter whether he went up or down the street. He had nothing to look for in either direction. He took off his grey-blue overcoat and slung it over his shoulder. He turned right and took the stone steps up towards the monastery.

Andrel wasn't looking for prayer. He wanted to escape the searing sun of the Italian town. He had only one pair of boots, excellent boots for winter in the east, high, black, made of cowhide, insulated with a felt lining. He would have liked to take them off and hurl them into the rapids of the Talfer River. In the cool interior of the Dominican church he found relief. He wiped the sweat from his neck with a handkerchief and headed for the San Giovanni Chapel, shaded and concealed at the side of the church.

There were several pews, but Andrel chose the carved prie-dieu. Who had prayed here before him? Whose whispers have pleased You over the centuries?

I'd been at the monastery just three months when I met him for the first time. Father Dominic of Clairvaux had visited before; now he was coming to our monastery permanently because he no longer had the strength to work. I took his meagre luggage to his cell. I showed Father to the office so he could report to the prior, in accordance with the rules, then to the library to leave his books, and to the nearby church. From that day on, he spent many long hours there. Leaning on the carved prie-dieu padded with a red cushion, he whispered: '*Et ne inducas me in tentationem.*' And lead me not into temptation. Only that. I used to watch him return alone to his cell. When he was still fit enough to leave the monastery on his own. That was before 1717.

Andrel leaned heavily against the pulpit as he struggled to his knees. His shirt was sticking to his back and he felt the need to change his underwear. He made the sign of the cross. A light was shining through the small stained-glass window just under the vault, illuminating the opposite wall. He looked up.
And froze.
The faces of the damned exhibited neither madness nor fear. Gold coiffed locks framed serious mouths and big blue eyes. The crimson robes and sky-blue sleeves fell softly, like silk. The damned turned their heads in longing, stretched

out their hands to the past. They had abandoned all hope, and yet they had not perished, they were still alive.

Those before them were drowning in the bottomless depths, burning in the fires of hell. But they stretched their hands backwards. Their horses, black, dapple-grey and auburn, their horses ahead, ahead, into a gallop, into the tousled mane, into the clatter of hooves, into the maelstrom of grey waters, into the gates of red flames. Who was chasing them? Who was giving them orders? The horses were carrying them straight to hell. Those in the flames, those in the maelstrom, all of them will perish. Hell is wide open. But they're looking to the past. Why?

Some women came into the church wearing colourful dresses. Only one was dressed in black. All of them had bags, wide hips and ample bosoms. They were talking loudly, they appeared to be comforting the one in black. They walked down the middle of the nave and went into the vestry. Would German women have behaved as improperly in the Church of St Nicholas in Halle where Klaus Weissmann had baptised his only son twenty-nine years ago?

A poppy-seed and rose loaf was cooling on the kitchen windowsill. Mother was making coffee. The godparents gave the child presents: a gold cross and a bracelet engraved with the name 'Andrel' and the date '30 May 1917'. For dinner they'd had potatoes, roast meat, lingonberries and gravy. The pickled plums had proved too strong to serve. Mother sliced the poppy-seed loaf to go with the coffee. Klaus Weissmann went to the dresser and brought out his home-made liqueur. The guests didn't leave their cosy flat on the second floor of the tenement house in the town centre until after dark.

On the first floor of the building lived a widow whose husband had perished in the Revolution, stabbed to death by bandits armed with knives. A few years later, Andrel sometimes wondered how many knives, but he never asked.

Johann Himlel, a piano teacher at the conservatory, had the ground-floor flat. He lived with his daughter and his son Joachim. Their mother was an actress who had left them at the first opportunity. From then on, Joachim started coming to Andrel's flat with his younger sister.

'What am I?' asked the seven-year-old Joachim with a devious grin. 'What am I: in the morning I walk on four legs, at noon on two, and in the evening on three?'

Andrel gave it some thought. Joachim laughed.

'A man, brother! A man! And this one? Where are there the most dry rivers?'

'In the desert,' shouted his younger sister.

Andrel grew sullen.

'I knew that.'

Joachim laughed.

'On the map. Right, last chance. What is the tomb of thoughts?'

Andrel racked his brain.

'Think, what is it: the tomb of thoughts?'

'I don't know. Tell me!'

'I'll tell you tomorrow.'

Sometimes, Andrel's mother would take Joachim's sister on to her lap, brush her thick hair and ask: 'Couldn't

I have had a daughter like you?' Then she would give them all sweets, after which Andrel had to brush his teeth with a disgusting paste.

Joachim Himlel went to two schools—one regular and one Jewish. He also took piano and violin lessons. Before he turned twelve, he started taking singing lessons with the cantor. On Saturdays he sang at the synagogue and he had no time for Andrel. Andrel suffered silently in his bedroom. He missed his friend very much. In the end, he decided he also wanted to study music. He begged his mother for so long that she agreed. She baked a poppy-seed loaf, wrapped it in a cloth, buttoned up her cardigan and went downstairs to see Mr Himlel. Andrel wanted to take lessons every day, but Klaus Weissmann, an arithmetic teacher at a German secondary school, didn't earn enough to pay the conservatory professor for five lessons a week. So Andrel went to Mr Himlel's on Wednesdays. After his lesson, he would stay a while longer to read music with Joachim. When he got home, he always heard his father muttering something about Germans being cheated, that they'd been stabbed in the back with a treacherous knife, and the master race had become the servants of Europe since the war. But he paid for the lessons.

Andrel loved those evenings with Joachim, who was older and wiser than him. He liked to listen to his stories about how he'd become a filmmaker one day. They pretended to make films together. Joachim was the cameraman and the director, Andrel was his best actor, playing all the roles—apart from the female ones, which were either unnecessary or could be played by Joachim's sister. It was really hard putting up with that girl. Andrel didn't understand why Joachim even brought her along with him, he'd have preferred to have Joachim to himself, especially once a week. Wednesday was his favourite day.

How long did Andrel spend there that Wednesday on the carved prie-dieu that had been polished by those who had prayed there over the centuries and gazed at Giotto's frescoes?

Someone had left a dog outside the church. The sun was setting in a blood-red glow behind the hillside vineyards. Andrel had no desire to return to the boarding house where he was staying for a few days on his way from German Tyrol to America. But he hadn't expected it to be so difficult to obtain a travel card. True, the Tyrolean man with whom he had spent the winter had suggested he get documents with a new name, he'd even offered to get the documents for him, but Andrel hadn't seen the need. He had absolutely nothing to be ashamed of. In principle, his job in the camp was bookkeeping for the fur farms, which he had clearly indicated on the form. Personally, he had opposed the liquidation of several thousand workers in November 1943, just when there was the most work and the highest volume of orders. He'd told his superior that. Because it was impossible to replace the workers overnight with a new transport of Jews. In peak season, in November, when the males have the most beautiful fur and the females' undercoats are at their thickest. When he recounted this, the Tyrolean man just shrugged.

After leaving the church, Andrel instinctively headed towards the river. He walked along the dirt road, then turned on to a well-trodden path through the undergrowth. He passed a couple having sex and sat down with his back against the central span of the bridge. There was no one in Bolzano who could confirm his identity. The more he thought about this, the more hopeless he felt. He threw some stones in the river and watched them disappear beneath the water's surface. The couple from the bushes had finished a while ago and left in the direction of the city. The cloudless, azure sky darkened. It was getting chilly. Andrel could feel the damp stretching out from the river. A shiver went through him. Then another. He hugged his knees, like he had as a child.

He used to sit on the windowsill in his bedroom and look down on to the street where they lived. The boys from the cheder would be walking down the middle of the road. Andrel searched for Joachim's silhouette, but when he saw how he was walking, swaying from side to side, how he was kicking a small stone and defending it from the others, how he kept his hands in his pockets and whistled between his teeth, Andrel felt a sharp pang of jealousy.

'I'd like to be you,' he'd said in a moment of sincerity the first time he played the entire score of *Moonlight Sonata* without mistakes.

Joachim just laughed and said, 'You don't know what you're saying.' He slid some sheets from the *Symphony of Psalms* on to the music shelf. 'And this? Can you play this?'

Andrel spent the entire evening poring over the notes.

In the final year of high school, it turned out that Joachim couldn't take the exams. He and a few other boys like him were expelled from the school. Andrel's father said, 'I wish you'd find yourself some better company,' but he didn't stop him going to the Himlels' for lessons. Not long after that, the piano teacher lost his job and suggested to Andrel's mother that he could give the boy three lessons a week. For the same price. From then on, Andrel played sonatas and études on Mondays, Wednesdays and Thursdays. And three times a week he spent a whole hour with Joachim. And his sister.

On Monday, Joachim's sister opened the door. Andrel went inside.

'They've taken our father,' she said, her lips quivering.

'And Joachim?' asked Andrel.

'He went to see him an hour ago,' she whispered, clinging suddenly to Andrel's sleeve.

'Hide me,' she whispered.

Andrel pushed her away, hissed, 'What are you thinking?' and escaped upstairs.

The next day, the ground-floor flat was empty.

Some men came to take the piano away.

It was slowly getting dark. His legs were numb and the damp from the river was penetrating through his T-shirt. He was freezing, but he didn't want to go back to the boarding house. He was stalling. Eventually, he decided to stop off at a local bar.

The sour smell of beer and urine hit him as he opened the door. The owner, a man with a short moustache, stood behind the bar, his hands spread wide on the bar top. He was standing still, watching everything around him closely. He didn't look like the friendly type.

Andrel asked for a beer. The barman didn't move an inch. Andrel repeated his order. The barman didn't even look at him. Andrel took out a banknote and placed it in front of the moustached man.

'From Tyrol?' came a voice from behind him in his native tongue.

'From Tyrol,' he confirmed automatically, before turning to see who was speaking.

It was a man the same height as him wearing an identical grey-blue overcoat and black cowhide boots. They must have been a similar age.

'Two,' he said brusquely to the barman, and pointed to a table by the wall.

They sat down. Clinked their beer mugs together. The other man took a packet of strong, reeking tobacco from his coat pocket. He offered it to Andrel. Andrel didn't refuse. He inhaled. He coughed. He felt dizzy.

'You're lying. You're not from Tyrol,' said the man in a thick northern accent. 'I know Germans from Tyrol. They drink differently, smoke differently.'

Andrel swiftly gained control of the panic rising inside him. Under no circumstances should this man become suspicious of the truth of his words.

'No, I'm from Halle,' he said, reaching into his coat pocket and taking out the crumpled form where everything was written clearly. 'But I came here from Tyrol.'

'*Ach so*,' sighed the man. 'So you're leaving too, like everyone else.'

'I don't know.' Andrel's temples were throbbing. He had a bitter taste in his mouth. He downed the rest of his beer. The next one was already on the table. 'I have to find two witnesses.'

'Two? Well, that's a bind. Because if you only needed one, you know, I could testify that you're you.'

'You could?' said Andrel, his eyes narrowed in distrust. 'For how much?'

'Why? Don't tell me you're not you,' said the man, laughing.

'I am me. But you don't even know my name.'

The man brought his rough hand down on the form lying in front of him on the dirty table.

'Andrel Weissmann?'

Andrel nodded. He felt as if his skull were cracking open.

'But it doesn't matter anyway, because you need two,' said the man.

'Yes, I need two because I don't have papers.'

'What bad luck. I've got papers and I'm not going anywhere.'

'Yeah?'

'Yeah.'

'Yeah…'

'Let's switch.'

'What?'

'Let's switch.'

'But how?'

'I'll be Andrel, you'll be Ondre. Your name will be my name.'

Andrel took in what the man was saying.

'Let's switch. You need papers, I have papers. Want them? Take them.'

'But how? Don't you need papers?'

'No.'

'Why not?'

'No.'

'No?'

'No. Everyone here has known me for centuries, right?' Ondre prodded a local who was sleeping with his head on his arm. 'Who am I?'

The local started, rubbed his eyes and examined him closely.

'What do you mean? You're Ondre Bianco, old Feher's son.'

'There you go! Here, let's smoke.'

Andrel held out a trembling hand for the cigarette. His temples felt like they were being gripped with a pair of pliers, a red-hot iron was gliding over his skin. His mouth filled with bile. Shudders were running through his body like before, at the river.

'I'll tell you how.' The man blew smoke right into his face. 'I'll tell you how. Tomorrow morning you'll go and show them my documents. Then they'll tell you to fill out a form. You write the truth. What's your name?'

'Andrel.'

'Good. You write Andrel, and write Ondre next to it, then they'll ask you which version of the name you use. Then they'll ask you why you entered Weissmann…'

'Weissmann? I should put Weissmann?'

'…and you reply that Bianco in German is Weissmann. That's all. And they'll ask you which version of your surname they should enter, and you say: Weissmann, because it means Bianco. That's what you tell them.'

'And they'll write that?'

'Yes.'

'OK,' said Andrel, stumbling to his feet to avoid vomiting on the table.

He stood outside, his legs wide apart, bent double. His guts lurched painfully. He felt as if he were going to puke up his own brain. Leaning against the wall, he touched his forehead with his other hand. It was ice-cold, although Andrel could feel his cheeks burning, his head was on fire, red-hot lava was running down his back and disappearing between his buttocks. He felt that he was dying. Ondre appeared at his side.

'Give me your hand, I'll help you, brother,' he said. His voice came from somewhere far away.

Father Dominic of Clairvaux died at the Dominican monastery. He hadn't left his cell in several months, and for the past week it had been feared that he was on the verge of death. He was certainly the oldest living monk in Bolzano. There were even rumours that he was over 100 years old, although his documents showed that he was only ninety-eight. In any case, he died. On Sunday after terce, Father Giovanni Battista held a short Holy Mass in the presence of his confrères with a prayer for all monks who had departed over the centuries. Then he visited Father Dominic in his cell, administered the viaticum in the form of bread and wine for his final journey, and anointed his thin, parchment-dry skin with holy oils.

'Ondre, keep me informed of his condition. If he refuses, call me immediately. Understood?' he said to me before he went to responsory. I was seventeen years old and Father Dominic was the first monk to whom I had been assigned for private service. I was excited about it.

The cells of the sick, old and dying were in the west wing. The prior had explained that the west symbolised the sloping of their lives which, like the sun, were dipping towards their time of rest.

So I stood in the corridor in front of the door to Father Dominic's cell and looked through the window. It was morning, but the sun didn't reach these rooms. A single bell was ringing somewhere outside. Half an hour passed. I stood and waited, but there was silence behind the wooden door.

By noon, my legs were aching. I crouched down opposite the cell door and leaned against the stone wall. The cold permeated to my core.

When the brothers gathered for nones, I quietly entered Father Dominic's cell. I hoped that the dying man was asleep and that I'd be able to leave him until mealtime. But he wasn't asleep. He was lying on his back, his head raised on a pillow. I looked at him closely. He had no hair. He looked like a wax figure.

'Do you need anything, Father?' I asked.

Father Dominic had stopped communicating some time ago. Perhaps he had even forgotten human language. So I didn't expect an answer to my question. Indeed, he didn't budge. I went closer to see if his bladder needed emptying.

I had taken care to empty his bowels in the morning before he received the sacraments. To do this, I had to position Father Dominic on his left side, facing the wall, bend his legs at the knees and pull up his nightshirt. It was cold in the cell, so Father Dominic's body immediately broke out in goose bumps. I covered him with a blanket. I left only the buttocks uncovered; I parted them gently and, holding them open with my left hand, I massaged Father Dominic's anus with my index finger. The shrivelled opening clenched, but I knew I had to be patient. To help it along, I used beef suet, which I'd asked Brother Angello to acquire from the kitchen. Brother Angello was full of sympathy for me.

After a while, the anus started to loosen. On a blanket nearby I'd prepared a small pair of bellows, just right for emptying a monk's bowels. When the time came, I first inserted my finger into Father's anus, getting the initial, most painful part out of the way. Then gradually, so as not to cause Father any pain, I inserted the hard leather tip of the bellows. I poured the medicinal fluid into his intestines as slowly as I could. Fortunately, the old monk appeared calm and relaxed, as if he were enjoying it, although it was merely a necessary procedure prior to taking the sacraments. The emptying of the bowels proceeded automatically on removal of the leather tip. I held Father's parted buttocks over the chamber pot. It wasn't hard. Then I rubbed his sunken stomach for a while, but withdrew my hand when I touched his protruding hip bones. I knew this place was sometimes painful for him. Despite the rubbing, I didn't manage to extract anything else from Father's insides. I wiped his anus with a damp cloth, pulled down his nightshirt, laid him on his back and covered him with the blanket.

When Father Giovanni Battista came into the cell carrying the Body of Christ, Father Dominic was lying there clean and ready. I was proud of him.

Now I had to put my cold hand under the blanket to see if Father needed to urinate. When his bladder was full, I had to get him the chamber pot.

By accident, I touched his small, dry hand under the blanket.

'Give me your hand, brother. I'll help you,' I said, not recognising my own voice. Echoing off the monastery walls, it came from somewhere far away.

Father's hand was as weak as a child's. I was now holding the hand of the oldest monk in Bolzano monastery, and he seemed to be squeezing back. Was it possible his fingers were clenching my hand? Apparently so. I stood over the dying old man with my hand in his, as if I were helping him cross to the other side. Father Dominic closed his eyes. He was so weak that he didn't open them again for a long time. After a while, he seemed to have fallen asleep. His breathing was shallow but calm. He was still alive. Was he sorry to be departing his long, holy life?

He was sitting in the drawing room of the art dealer Hendrick van Uylenburgh. There was a small coffee table covered with a lace tablecloth, and next to the table a lamp with an intricate lampshade. As evening fell and the curtains were drawn, a footman came in to light the candles. Father Dominic of Clairvaux didn't notice when Rembrandt—presumably some distant relative of Hendrick's—entered the room. He didn't move to make space for the newcomer. He seemed to be engrossed in conversation with Johannes de Renialme. The Eighty Years' War had just ended, and shipping had started up in all directions. Father Dominic travelled widely on behalf of His Holiness Pope Innocent X. Throughout the 1640s, the Office of the Inquisition had demanded considerable commitment. And Father Dominic's experience and the strength of his arguments made him extremely effective.

Hendrick asked the footman to bring another chair. Rembrandt sat down and placed a small etching on the table. It had been made on thick, coarse paper, but that didn't matter. It showed a man with a birdlike profile bent over a map that emitted a hypnotic glow. Hendrick van Uylenburgh reached for it first. Andreas Bianco's face was twisted in a sharp grimace, but Father Dominic knew this had nothing to do with the etching. He examined it and saw what he was afraid to see. His Holiness would have given all the treasures of the Vatican for that map. Father Dominic could see why.

He didn't manage to speak to Rembrandt that evening, but from then on, Father Dominic was always seeking a way to ask him in person about the map he had rendered so faithfully in his etching. It couldn't have been a coincidence. Father Dominic wanted to find out everything about that map, even if he had to use his position to do so. Before the Pope found out about it, of course.

I stood motionless over the old man's bed so as not to wake him. I was still holding his hand beneath the warm blanket. After a while my back started aching, so to get some relief I knelt down very carefully beside the bed. I knelt like that for a long time, and finally I laid my head gently on the pillow next to Father Dominic's. I know it was inappropriate, but there was no one else in the cell other than him. It was the first time I'd seen another person so very, very close. I could even see the white hairs in his ear. A few patches of grey stubble on his cheeks. Wisps of steam escaping his nostrils and his sunken lips slightly parted. I wanted to pray, but I felt too tired. Can you be too tired to pray? My eyes were stinging, and I found relief in closing them frequently. I knelt in this odd position, breathing in the rhythm of his breath and drawing warmth from his weakening hand. My eyes stayed closed for longer and longer, the periods of alertness grew shorter. My thoughts began to slip away from me, into the past, of which there was no certainty, or the future, which after all may never happen.

I was kneeling like that by Father's bed when, suddenly, I felt that someone had entered the room. I wanted to wake up, but I didn't have the strength. Someone was searching Father Dominic's cell. He came over to the bed and stood over the two of us for a long time, studying the old monk lying on his back with his hands under the blanket, and me, a young boy kneeling in an odd position with his head on the dying man's pillow. Then he left. His hobnailed cowhide boots clattered against the stone flooring. I counted his steps until they faded away, muffled by the monastery walls.

The sun had not yet risen when the bell called the brothers to lauds. The shuffling of their feet was audible as they walked in two uneven lines towards the dark, cold church. I was hungry. I could feel a sucking in my stomach, my left arm had gone numb, and the pain in my knees was unbearable. Gently I drew my hand out from under the blanket, stood up and urinated into the chamber pot. I glanced at Father over my shoulder. His eyes were open. I was terribly ashamed to be urinating in the face of death, but I couldn't stop. All I could do in that situation was avert my gaze from the dying man. As soon as I'd finished, I knelt down beside him. Father Dominic's lips were moving as if he were whispering the words of a psalm.

'*Deus, in adiutorium meum intende, Domine, ad adiuvandum me festina.*' Make haste, O God, to deliver me; make haste to help me, O Lord. '*Deus, in adiutorium meum intende, Domine, ad adiuvandum me festina. Deus, in adiutorium meum intende, Domine, ad adiuvandum me festina,*' he whispered.

I began reciting the words of the psalm with him.

At some point, Father Dominic turned his face towards me and said very softly, 'I know where hell is. I've seen it.'

I brought my ear close to his mouth so as not to miss a word.

'I stole it, I hid it.'

I was kneeling right beside him. I could hear every syllable.

'In a black coffin lined with red velvet. I hid it. In the tomb of thoughts.'

Father's hands were trembling, tears running down his grey cheeks. He looked like a child. Old Father Dominic had lost his mind. He was talking nonsense. I stroked his head.

'I've seen it. It's there, the gate of hell. Find it and destroy it.' His voice was weak but audible.

I nodded. What else could I do?

'Yes, Father.' I kept stroking his head.

'My memories will be your memories. Do you understand?'

'Yes, Father.'

The old man's breathing grew steady, his tears dried. His breathing was increasingly slow and shallow. He seemed to have fallen asleep. I knelt by his bed for a long, long time until I noticed Father was no longer warm.

'*Requiem aeternam dona eis, Domine, et lux perpetua luceat eis. Requiescant in pace.* Amen.'

No sooner had I said 'Amen' than the cell door swung open. Brother Angello was standing there with a bowl of soup.

'He has gone in the peace of Christ,' I said, passing him in the doorway.

The old German man checked the time on his phone. He rose from the prie-dieu and made his way out of the chapel. As he passed the verger, he smiled and handed him twenty euros. He didn't have any smaller notes, he'd forgotten to get change. The verger put the note in his back pocket. There was something familiar about that boy. In his eyes, the shape of his shaved head. How old could he be? Seventeen?

'Have you seen the crypt beneath the monastery? I know where the side entrance is,' said the boy, winking.

It was already late when they descended the steep, stone steps to the small basement.

'There's nothing to be scared of here,' whispered the boy, turning to the old man. 'They died centuries ago.'

The air in the crypt was dry and smelled of limestone. Small coffins were lined up along the walls, from floor to ceiling, on scaffolding that resembled bookcases. Andrel walked over to one of the coffins and wiped away the dust with his hand. Through the rotten wood of the lid, it was possible to see inside. Padre Dominique di Chiaravalle 1617–1717. A narrow coffin lay next to it on the same shelf: Confrater Ondre 1700–1717. Ondre. The seventeen-year-old with no surname and the centenarian padre had died the same year.

'Dominic of Clairvaux, the Inquisitor known in seventeenth-century Europe for his cruelty, spent his final years in our monastery,' said the verger. 'Some of the coffins are empty,' he added. 'I checked. They must have been laid to rest over there.' The boy pointed to an alcove at the back.

Andrel Weissmann walked past the stacked coffins into the darkness. Beneath the clay wall he discovered a pit full of human bones covered in scraps of rotted cloth. He knew that image. For a moment, he thought he saw legs covered in brown stockings.

'Let's get out of here.'

They left.

He stood for a long time leaning against the ruined monastery wall, breathing deeply.

'Are you feeling OK?' The boy looked into his black eyes with concern. And he stepped back in horror.

I knew where to look for the prior. If Father Giovanni Battista wasn't praying or holding Mass, he was either in his cell or in the reading room. This time he was in his cell.

'Father Dominic has died,' I said without meeting his eye.

'How did he depart?'

'In the peace of Christ. At the end, evil confounded his mind and tongue.'

'Did he say something?'

I nodded.

'What?'

'That he had found the path to hell. And that he had a map that leads to its gates.'

Father Giovanni looked up at me, standing there before him in the doorway and claiming that Father Dominic had regained the ability to speak on his deathbed and had confessed to me, an uninitiated youth, something he had kept secret his whole life.

Father Giovanni looked closely at this boy who was not even in the novitiate yet, despite his zealous participation in monastery life. His eyes were shining and his cheeks were flushed; he looked unwell.

'Father Dominic went in peace,' said Ondre.
'Do you remember his words?'
'He was delirious, Father.'
'You didn't answer my question.'
Ondre lowered his head.
'Yes, Father.'
'Repeat.'
He repeated.
Father Giovanni fell silent. He looked out of the window for a long time. A bird was perched on a bare branch.
'What is the tomb of thoughts?' he asked, not expecting an answer.
'He didn't say, Father.'
'You may go.'

I left. I was so tired, I felt nothing. When I reached my cell, I collapsed on to my bed without taking off my habit and wrapped myself tightly in the blanket. But I didn't feel any warmer.

I dreamed that someone was searching my cell, and then Father Dominic lay down beside me and slipped under the blanket. He moved his cold body against mine and whispered into my ear through stiffening lips: 'Move over. Come on, move over, I'm falling.' I felt that I was falling with him.

In a temporary, hastily prepared room across the hall from the Holy Office, a woman in a black dress was kneeling, beating her chest with her fists and crying repeatedly that her son had copulated with the devil and then spat out the Body of Christ. He had choked on it and spat it out. The blessed sacrament had grown and grown in his mouth, filled his throat and tried to invade his lungs and deeper, into his guts, the pious woman declared.

She was like all the other women Ondre knew. One minute her face was clear, the next it lost its contours. He tried to focus his gaze and grasp hold of the details, but the more he tried, the more the image faded and blurred, and he was no longer sure if it was a woman or Father Dominic, or this boy who was standing in front of him now. He was older and wiser than Ondre. He knew the answers to all questions. Confident as hell. He kept his hands in the pockets of his loose trousers, tied with a narrow leather belt at the waist. He answered all Father Dominic's questions. He didn't confess to anything.

First, they shaved his head. The thick curls fell to the ground. Soon the floor around the chair on which he was sitting was covered with his hair.

Then they told him to strip naked. To fold his clothes and remember where they were.

The two men pushed him into the basement and left. Father Dominic appeared at the door. He was standing bolt upright in boots and black gloves. His white habit lay differently from usual on his frame. Perhaps because it was pulled in tightly at the waist with a buckle inscribed with gothic lettering.

The boy lay naked on the ground; he cowered and retreated to the far corner, but Father dragged him into the light. He had to carry out an inspection. He had to see with his own eyes whether there were any signs of Satan on him. Whether an impure spirit had left its marks on his skin. He examined his head, neck, shoulders and underarms. Elbows and hands. Stomach and ribs. Genitalia, foreskin, testes, groin. Legs. Backs of the knees. Feet. Nape of the neck, back, buttocks. He parted them with one hand in the black leather glove. The skin of the perineum tore, a drop of blood ran down. Father caught it on his thumb and sniffed. It reeked of hell.

The Inquisitor reached for the wooden pincers. He slid them between the boy's buttocks and opened his anus. It was red and scratched.

Father Dominic looked him in the eye. At this look, the boy began to tremble as if he had a fever. He wasn't confident now. He was afraid. He was afraid of divine justice. The providential eye of the Inquisition.

The two men entered at dawn. They were carrying a small brown suitcase, a bucket for waste and a bottle of oil. Father Dominic, wearing leather gloves and a black leather apron to protect his habit, set up an oil burner, put a small pot on top and poured in the oil. He waited for the oil to heat up, while the other two tied the boy's hands with a rope and threw him to the floor. He lay on his stomach, his nose bleeding. His legs were spread wide.

Father Dominic took a small pair of bellows from the suitcase.

Ondre was tossing and turning in his sleep. He knew those bellows, he recognised them, knew what they were for. He didn't want to know more.

Meanwhile, Father Dominic was drawing in the hot oil. Using the pincers, he opened the boy's anus again and poured the contents of the bellows inside.

Ondre let out an animal-like howl. He was still wailing when he woke up. His voice echoed in the monastery's silence as Brother Angello raced into his cell. He must have been loitering in the hall outside his door.

Ondre was panting, unable to speak. Angello laid a compress on his forehead and left the room. Ondre lay with his eyes wide open, trying with all his might not to close them, but his pupils soon began to sink into the depths, he was being consumed by the fever inside him. He wasn't sure of anything any more.

On the third day, the boy confessed to everything. When Father Dominic summoned him before the Holy Office, he was unable to stand.

'We'll extinguish your pain, my son,' said Father Dominic. 'With holy water.'

That night, Father entered the boy's cell alone. The moon was shining through the bars in the high window.

'Don't be afraid,' he said.

The boy was afraid. Father turned him over on to his stomach. All night long, he was given holy water. Drop by drop. By enema, using the same bellows Father had used for years, the bellows that had served him so well. Drop by drop. A whole bucket.

When Ondre began wailing, Brother Angello changed the compress on his forehead.

By morning the boy was swollen, his lips and tongue were black and he looked like a drowned body, but he didn't release a single drop of the holy water.

'The impurity has left you, my boy.'

That same day, the Inquisitor pronounced his sentence. In his infallibility, he acknowledged that the boy was possessed, but not entirely, just his tongue—the tongue that had spat out the blessed Body of Christ. The rest had been cleansed through the process of the Holy Inquisition. The only instruction was that his mother, who had brought to life this impure spawn, be burned at the stake.

During the execution, the boy meekly put his head between the metal clamps and the executioner cut off his tongue with a single blow. Father Dominic was moved.

Ondre fell into an unrelenting delirium. He bit his fingers till they bled; his lips cracked from the fever and took on a scarlet hue. His big eyes roamed vacantly across the walls. The horses were carrying him straight into the maelstrom of death. He raved and cried out in his sleep.

'A waste of a boy,' said Angello, feeding him with a spoon. 'So young.'

But he tossed his head, spilling the remains of the soup.

Sometimes Ondre would lie still, his eyes fixed on one point. But Angello had learned not to look into his eyes. He was afraid of what he might see there.

When Andrel woke the next morning, he was at the boarding house. How had he got there, and when? As he opened his eyes, pain rushed through his pupils into his skull. He squeezed his eyelids shut, but they didn't provide much shelter from the Italian sun. Snippets of conversation from the night before pulsated in his head. They swirled around him, but he couldn't catch hold of them.

'Let's switch, why not?' 'My memories will be your memories.' 'What is the tomb of thoughts?'… 'I'll tell you tomorrow.' 'Come on, switch, let's switch.' 'Move over, I'm falling.' 'You know how a camp is liquidated?'… 'I know how a ghetto is liquidated.' 'Alois Adler was a good doctor.' 'You know where his collection of foetuses ended up?'… 'I'll tell you tomorrow.' 'Will you leave?'… 'But how?'… 'I'll tell you tomorrow.'

Andrel looked at his watch. It was almost nine. He needed to join the queue for the emigration office. Time was running out. He quickly washed his face, armpits and crotch in the basin next to the wardrobe. He was afraid the landlady could walk in at any moment. He was tucking his shirt into his trousers when she knocked on the door.

'Are you leaving today?' she asked, looking around the room.

'We'll see,' he replied, not wishing to engage her in further conversation. He ran down the stairs and out on to the street. There was a long queue outside the emigration office.

Andrel queued for several hours. Once he was inside the dark, windowless corridor he reached into his coat pocket. Rather than a handkerchief, he found some documents. Two grease-stained cards, frayed at the corners and worn along the fold lines. One was the birth certificate of Ondre Bianco, the other his residence card.

'Name?' asked the glum official in the room filled with grey files.

Andrel handed him the documents. Completely authentic documents. The official slowly examined the papers, then gave Andrel a form and an indelible pencil and explained how to fill it out.

'Which version of your first name will you be using for your trip?' he asked.

'Andrel.'

'Why have you entered Weissmann as your surname?'

'Because Bianco is the same as Weissmann.'

'So what should I put for your surname?'

'Weissmann.'

'You're German,' he confirmed.

'I'm German.'

The official issued the travel document. The whole thing took seven minutes.

Andrel returned to the boarding house.

'Are you leaving today or paying for another night?' asked the landlady.

'I'm leaving,' said Andrel over his shoulder. He picked up his luggage, returned his key and went out on to the street.

He didn't remember much from the night before. He tried to refresh his memory about what he'd done, what he'd talked about with that man after leaving the bar, but it gave him a headache. For a few hours he wandered aimlessly around Bolzano. His shadow was either behind him or two steps ahead. He passed the bombed-out fourteenth-century cathedral. Without meaning to, he found himself outside Ondre's home. He stood for a long time under his window, but nothing happened. He decided to return to the Dominican church, but on the way he stopped off at a bar, sat down and drank two shots of vodka. Then he went to the river. He kicked the central span of the bridge, threw some stones in the water.

His heavy cowhide boots clattered loudly as he entered the San Giovanni Chapel. He collapsed on to the carved prie-dieu padded with a red cushion. Relief. He looked up. The damned were still on their way to perdition.

'What is the tomb of thoughts?' he heard from behind him in his native language.

He turned abruptly. Ondre was leaning against the whitewashed wall. A ray of sunlight fell from a small, high stained-glass window, illuminating his silhouette. Andrel could see only his contours.

'Think. Where do you bury thoughts? Where are philosophy and literature buried away?' Joachim smiles and nudges him in the ribs with his elbow.

'You promised you'd tell me,' says Andrel reproachfully. He'd give anything for Joachim to nudge him like that again.

'In the library, brother, in the library.' Joachim's laugh is short and bright. 'Here, try *Requiem*.'

Andrel squinted.

'Is that you, Ondre?'

Ondre peeled himself off the whitewashed wall of the San Giovanni Chapel.

'It's dangerous to assume the identity of a stranger these days,' he said, and plunged his knife between Andrel's ribs. He reached into Andrel's coat pocket and took the travel document issued with today's date in the name of Andrel Weissmann, born in Halle, Germany, baptised there in the Church of St Nicholas on 30 May 1917. He left the two grease-stained cards—the birth certificate and residence card—in the coat pocket.

He didn't have long, and he still needed to visit the ruins of the monastery library. He knew what to look for.

Blue moonlight streamed into the library through the holes in the ceiling. It was as clear as day. The steady patter of cowhide boots echoed down the hallway.

The man in the long leather overcoat pushed the door open with his shoulder. The heavy hinges groaned. A bird flew out from under the remains of the ceiling and swept up into the cold, dark-blue sky with a piercing shriek. Bare bookcases in the alcoves along the walls. Someone had diligently emptied them hundreds of years ago. This didn't concern him. He walked over to the cathedral and knelt down. The old floorboards creaked. He placed both hands over them, swept aside the layer of dust, halting at the bumps and cracks, prising them apart with his fingernails. In the pale moonlight, his face looked almost soulful. Finally, he heaved a sigh of relief and lifted the lid hidden in the podium. He plunged his arms in elbow-deep and took out a six-foot-long black tube bearing the papal seal.

In the morning, Ondre bought a ticket from Bolzano to Halle, where he would receive a certificate of baptism in his new name from the Church of St Nicholas. With a spring in his step, he boarded the train. He was carrying very little luggage.

It was the end of March 1946. Many like him were coming home.

The Hospital

The psychiatric hospital was not the kind of place you'd want to leave.

That's precisely why I chose it. It was located in the middle of a huge park, surrounded by trees and flower beds. I was convinced that was the best thing I could do for her. I'd promised to come and visit, and I kept my word. Every Sunday I parked my car in the driveway, which was covered in tiny black and white pebbles, I walked through the wrought-iron gate, nodded to the receptionist and entered her world. Sometimes I took the child along, so he could have some contact with his mother. But I usually visited alone.

The paths ran in concentric circles intersected by four, eight, sixteen crossroads. It was quite possible to see the hospital and not be able to reach it. Or you could be going in a completely different direction and suddenly, unexpectedly, the building was looming right in front of you. In this respect, it really didn't matter which path you took. A seeming detour might turn out to be the most direct route.

My weekly efforts to get to the hospital left me a bit flustered. I worried that someone would think I'd lost my way, so I strolled slowly along the gravel paths as if I had simply come here for a walk, or as if I were a doctor here, a professor perhaps, who was just keeping an eye on everything. I unbuttoned my overcoat, pushed my hat to the back of my head. I clasped my hands behind my back. People in pyjamas, dressing gowns and felt slippers were sitting on the benches. They stared blankly, some of them gazing into the distance with their mouths open. Every now and then, nurses appeared from among the trees wearing starched white caps with a black rim. They didn't look in my direction. They knew I wasn't a doctor, I could hardly be a professor, they knew I was here because I had to be. They knew.

The hospital consisted of several modernist pavilions, which had apparently been designed at the start of the twentieth century by renowned visionary and urban planner Hermann Stübben. The pavilions were arranged in the shape of the letter H. H for Hermann. Separate and slightly to the side was a semi-ruined chapel. As far as I could tell, Mass was held there on religious holidays and some of the patients prayed there during the week.

Pavilion C was right in the middle. It was a wide, three-storey building with staircases and lifts. Its windows faced south-west on one side and north on the other. My wife was on the first floor in the left wing, on the north-facing side. The manic depressives had more light, because they were on the first floor on the right. The paranoid schizophrenics were on the second floor. The canteen and doctors' offices were on the ground floor.

The system of stairs and lifts was rather complicated for visitors. There were no floor numbers in the lifts. Furthermore, there were several miniature lifts for transporting meals. For this reason I usually took the stairs, but that was no guarantee of success either. Some of the staircases led to the upper floors, others were connected to the adjacent pavilions, and still others ended unexpectedly in locked doors or walls.

If my wife happened to be feeling well and the weather was good, we went to the park and sat on the nearest bench in silence. I'd light a cigarette, but she wasn't allowed to smoke—the nicotine interacted with her medication and had a stimulating effect.

This had been explained to me by the psychiatrist, Doctor Adolf Orłowski, a bearded, middle-aged man. One day he'd invited me into his office. He spoke at length in such a low, calm voice that I almost fell asleep. I'd had a few sleepless nights lately, we'd been sent some kids from the technical college. It was hard work. I didn't want to hurt them, I really didn't, so I'd told Krasicki to leave them alone; he was indispensable when we needed to break or humiliate someone, because he exuded aristocracy and superiority. We named him Prince Bishop.

The other was Zwoleński, and I was equally scared of leaving the kids in his care. He had generations of persecution on his shoulders and tended to put up a fight. So I preferred to stay and talk with the students myself. They cracked one by one, but I was the truly exhausted one by the end of it. I didn't sleep at all on the Friday night. On the Saturday night I slept on a fold-out bed, then in the morning I washed my face, got dressed in my regular clothes and came straight here. All I dreamed of was sitting on a bench and lighting a cigarette. And no one talking to me. But I ran into the doctor, who invited me up to his office. We went inside. The doctor led me to a lift I'd never seen before. It must have been meant for only one person, it was so narrow and cramped. So we stood facing each other, self-conscious in each other's presence. I'd never been that close to another man before. I felt awkward. I avoided eye contact, he stared down at the floor. I fixed my eyes on the wall just above his head. The lift soon came to a halt with a slight rattle.

We had to go down the corridor. Between the windows, potted ferns and grasses with long shoots were hanging from the ceiling. On the opposite wall, reproductions of Bosch, Rembrandt, Van Gogh, Bruegel, Goya and Picasso. Rembrandt's *Faust* was hanging by the door to the doctor's office. I recognised it. As the doctor unlocked the door, it seemed to me that Faust was giving me a dirty look, a look of disapproval. We went inside. The doctor invited me to sit in the armchair, and he took a seat behind the desk.

The office was floating in the liquid amber of September sun. A fly drunk on happiness dozed between the window-panes. The shelves were heaving with volumes on psycho-analysis. Little stacks of sick notes and Diazepam prescriptions on the desk. A pencil case with a zipper, like a sleeping bag. A soft leather armchair for taking naps. And the low, soothing voice of the psychiatrist reassuring me that while my wife's condition was serious, the drugs were working, explaining that nicotine is a stimulant, that she might be let out for Christmas, but it wasn't guaranteed. My eyelids were leaden, the lead weighed heavy in my breast pocket too and pulsed in my temples. The doctor played with his lighter, which was shaped like a revolver. There was a pot on the desk filled with pens and sharpened pencils. The sun was pinning me to the chair.

'Are you feeling all right?'

'I'm sorry. I've had a lot of work on lately.'

'I understand.'

From the look he gave me, I saw that he really did understand. I felt that no one had understood me as well as he did in that moment. The sun was pouring its warmth through the window; I didn't want to leave.

'Your wife is being well looked after,' he said.

'She was very lucky to end up here,' I replied.

Technically, I could have got up then, shaken the doctor's sturdy hand and left, but he made no gesture to indicate the conversation was over—on the contrary, he seemed interested in what I had to say, as if he was waiting for something more. Besides, I didn't want to lift my body up out of the armchair and go out into the courtyard flooded in afternoon sun. I wanted to sit there amid the dreamy decor and finally tell someone, show someone my whole life.

'I met her after the war,' I started awkwardly, breaking the long silence. The doctor looked at me attentively. 'I was twenty years old and so was she. I was doing fieldwork, she worked in propaganda. One day, I brought a bunch of wildflowers to her office. Her friends were so jealous. I rode a motorcycle, she walked. I gave her a lift once, then a second time. She invited me in for tea. I stayed the night. I was single, and so was she. We invited all our friends and her family to the wedding. Six people. For the first year after the wedding we lived in a workers' hostel. We ate separately, she in the canteen, I in the field. She didn't ask about anything, neither did I. In the evenings I'd come home tired, have a wash in a bowl in the hallway and lie down next to her on the sofa bed. We had sex. Quite regularly. After a year, she fell pregnant. The child was born healthy, but she... She changed a lot after that. She retreated, reacted disproportionately to things. When I wanted to have sex with her, she'd burst out laughing. Hysterical, unrestrained, deranged laughter. She'd laugh until she couldn't breathe. Until she lost consciousness. I'd beg her to stop, but she didn't listen. In the end, I had to hit her. To make her come to her senses. Not too hard. If I'd wanted to, I would have hit her hard, right? The next day, she bought some dark glasses with my money. She looked like a film star. They were very flattering.

'Her problems started getting worse. She smacked her lips while eating and slurped her tea. It bothered me, so I forbade her from eating in my presence. She had to go out to the toilet in the corridor. We were living in a workers' hostel. There was only one shared toilet. Our relationship normalised and it seemed that everything would be OK. Unfortunately, my wife's condition soon took a turn for the worse. She completely stopped looking after herself. On Saturdays, I made her strip naked and I poured water over her. She didn't like that. By Friday evening, she'd be promising to pull herself together. She didn't always keep her word.

'I noticed that lack of sleep did her good. When she hadn't slept much, she didn't burst out laughing in that way of hers, and she didn't get breathless. She was calmer, and she took better care of the baby. So I set the alarm clock every forty minutes for her own good. I suspect, though, that she was catching up on sleep during the day when I was at work and couldn't keep an eye on her.

'Then the nightmares started. She'd jump out of bed screaming, waking me and the entire hostel. It was extraordinary. As an investigating officer I'd often heard screams coming from the interrogation room—I knew what it takes to make a person scream. But the noise she came out with was beyond human comprehension.

'You can imagine what my life was like during that time. Everything I did, I did for her sake. I tried not to bring my work methods home, I really tried, but sometimes it was impossible. As a result, I didn't feel like working, nor coming home. I felt like my life was losing all meaning. Do you know that feeling?'

Doctor Orłowski reached for the penknife he used to open ampoules and started to clean his fingernails with it. He glanced at me again and again over the rims of his thick glasses. His eyes were remarkable. He listened without saying a word.

Do you believe it's possible not to die? I don't mean immortality, just the possibility of not dying. That you can want something so much that... That you won't... That you won't die.

One day, a man in his eighties came up to me and asked to speak to me in private. He said his father couldn't die, because he'd promised himself he wouldn't die until he found out what had happened to his cow. He'd had a black and white cow. It was a good black and white cow that had been allocated to a State collective farm. The man's father had even wanted to buy it back from the State, but it had disappeared without a trace. And he'd vowed not to die. According to the man, his father was 120 years old and suffering greatly. So I put on my uniform, picked up my briefcase and went to see him.

I pull up in front of his house and I see someone chopping wood. I go over, I enquire. It's him. I ask how old he is. 'One hundred and twenty,' he says, leaning on the butt of the axe. Then I open my briefcase and take out some documents. 'I'm from the Ministry. I have a cow transfer deed for you. One black and white cow. Due to the fact that the cow is dead, you will receive the monetary equivalent,' I say, and I shell out the money, like his son and I agreed. 'When did she die?' he asks. 'October 7,' I say, not batting an eyelid. He nods, puts down the axe and goes into the house. His son called me later to say his father had lain down on the bed in the kitchen, his shoes still on, and died. I went to his funeral.

But why am I saying this. It's pointless.

It's pointless to tell you this. Let's get back to my wife. I don't know what her behaviour would have led to.

My life became a nightmare because of her. I might even have ended it all. That's the way I was starting to think.

The turning point came one day when we were searching the house of someone we'd brought in for interrogation. I came across a black and white photograph. On the back, written in pencil, was a place name and a date: April 1940. A very good photograph. Faces razor-sharp. High contrast. White patches of sunlight, dark shadows. Women standing in a line on a big square with a well in the middle. Their white bodies. Naked. Their black pubic hair. They're facing a man in a black overcoat. His eyes are closed, his face turned towards the sun. His white face and the flock of black birds against the cloudless sky. The women are looking at the birds. They're looking at the birds as if they're raising their prayers to God. His eyes are closed.

In the background of the photograph is a small hut. A second man stands in the half-open door, a white coat over his uniform. A blurred figure, out of focus.

But the most important element was in the foreground. The bare shoulders and face of my mother. In the foreground, first on the right, her face. I recognised her. She was standing in line. Naked, her head shaved, but I'd recognise her face anywhere.

It was the first time I'd seen my mother's face in many years. Do you understand?

I'd last seen her in early October when she put on a dress and went to work. She didn't come back. The more I waited for her, the more she didn't come back.

A month earlier they'd shot my father. Outside the Jesuit church. Right in front of me. I stood and watched his death. The evening before, he'd beaten me with a leather belt in front of our neighbour. He told me to take off my trousers. Then Father tanned my hide. I was burning with shame all night; the words of my prayers caught in my throat. I wished death on him, I wanted him to die. And the next day when they shot all the teachers, him included, I felt no regret. I felt nothing. Two towers made of white stone stretched the black stumps of their charred beams up into the sky. All for nothing.

The doctor opened the window and took out some cigarettes. The drowsy fly twitched its wings and settled again on the white net curtain. We lit up. The sunlight warmed my back.

There were seventy naked women in the photograph, my mother, the man in the black overcoat and the other man in the white coat. Who were they? Do you want to know?

My research was thorough. My investigator's ID card opened every door to me, both here and abroad. I dressed in civilian clothes, you know, corduroy jacket, tinted glasses, a small shoulder bag. They gave me a passport for the Socialist Bloc. And off I went. I travelled across East Germany, Czechoslovakia and the Hungarian People's Republic. The whole of Yugoslavia. I identified one of them with little trouble in Sarajevo. He was in some of the other photographs. Always in the women's camps. Always in a black overcoat, always with his face turned towards the sun. His name was

Andrija, but he also signed as Ondre. I became a graphology expert when it came to his signature. I saw his signature thousands of times. I got hold of the remains of his journal. I know everything about him. I know nothing about him.

His signature was also on my mother's deportation order. I went there. Of course I went there. I took the photograph with me.

I found the square with the well. I found the concrete hut. In the town hall nearby, I found a memorial plaque showing the number of victims of the murderous experiments. No names. I didn't find my mother's name anywhere. I didn't find a single name of any of those women whose transport was escorted by Andrija.

I went into the town hall and requested access to all documents from the 1940s. My request was met with silent disapproval, but after I showed my ID they ushered me along a corridor that led behind the stairs. The corridor sloped downwards. Its ceiling was dangerously low in several places. A young man with a black moustache and a bunch of keys walked in front of me. We turned a few corners. It was cold, I could feel the musty damp on my face. I don't know if I could have found my way back on my own.

The man opened a heavy metal door, revealing several tall rows of shelving crammed with grey files. I picked up the first one that came to hand, raising a cloud of dust right in front of my face. The man seemed to heave a sigh and say something like, 'Always the same.' Then louder: 'You see, I told you there was nothing worth looking for here.'

What was I looking for? What did I expect to find?

From then on, I visited the archive daily.

Andrija only transported pregnant women. Selected women. In the photograph they stood in order from six to nine months. What was my mother doing among them? Her name wasn't there. The *Name* column showed the race, age and size of the foetus. In millimetres and grams.

The doctor's faded signature underneath. He used black ink. Adler.

The doctor was playing with a fountain pen, white with a glossy sheen. He looked towards the window. The disc of the sun was balanced on the treetops, ready to tumble backwards, plunging the world into darkness. My wife must have returned to the ward by now. It was almost dinnertime.

Time was against me. I knew the doctor's full name, I knew his exact address. He came from Hoboken in Antwerp. I bought a map of the city and found the street where he lived. I even marked the shortest route from the station. I imagined every mile, every turn I'd need to take. I saw him standing in the dark doorway of his house dressed in his white coat; I've imagined it hundreds of times. I tell him my mother's name, he turns pale, his eyes widen, he takes two steps back, clutches at his heart and falls to the ground. I stand over him and stamp his white face into the black earth.

Unfortunately, there was no chance for me to travel to the West before the end of the 1960s. Nor in the early 1970s.

So by the time I got a passport and crossed the border, it was already late.

I drove all the way there, pulling up right outside his gate. It was autumn, dusk was falling. The entry gate was closed. I had to get out of the car. It was starting to rain, so I turned up my coat collar and pulled my hat down over my ears. I walked through a large garden, probably once magnificent, now neglected. The stone statues had crumbled over time. They stood there without noses, following me with empty eye sockets. The rain trickled down their cheeks. The driveway was strewn with broken branches. Even if the gate had been open, there was no way my car could have got past them.

A sleepy maid answered the door. She was wearing a light-coloured housecoat, and a starched bonnet over her hair. I don't remember her name. Maybe she didn't tell me. I said I was looking for Doctor Adler. That I'd come a long way specially to see him. That he was an acquaintance of my mother's and I wanted to talk to him. That it was very urgent and extremely important to me. She looked at me, at my wet overcoat, at the garden behind, and showed me inside. She told me to take a seat in the circular entrance hall, from which a grand black staircase led up to the first floor. I sat down beside a little chess table and waited. After about fifteen minutes, the maid returned with a cup of tea. She put it down in front of me. Then she pulled up a chair and sat next to me.

'He's dead,' she said. 'He died a long time ago.'

I didn't say anything.

'You can stay until the morning if you like. There are spare rooms upstairs. Best not to go back in the middle of the night.'

I couldn't believe he'd escaped me so easily.

The maid led me upstairs and showed me to my room. She closed the door and I didn't see her again after that.

I sat on the bed. Water was dripping from my coat, but I didn't have the strength to take it off. Still wearing my shoes and hat, I lay down on the fresh sheets. I thought I was awake, that my eyes were open and I was fully conscious, but I must have fallen asleep after all because I was woken by the chiming of the clock in the entrance hall. It was half past something. I wasn't sure of the hour because I'd left my watch at home, in the drawer beside the bed. Stupid of me, but never mind. I got up, feeling stiff all over. I opened the door quietly and went to the end of the hall. I didn't find the toilet, but I stumbled upon a narrow, steep staircase leading up to the attic, and down to the servants' quarters and the cellars. The stairs to the attic were cluttered with junk, so I decided to go down to the basement. On the way down I passed a dark kitchen. At that point, the stone steps twisted into a spiral and became even steeper. I groped about for a light switch. A weak bulb lit up the space below me. I went in that direction.

I was descending for a long time, though I don't know if it was because the staircase was so long or because I was going so slowly. When I reached the bottom, I found myself in front of a door made of wooden planks. There was a twenty-inch gap between the top of the door and the wall. I hoisted myself up with ease, slung my legs up and squeezed through the opening.

On the other side was a stone cellar, the walls lined with shelves full of winter preserves. The jars with glass lids, rubber seals and metal clasps must have been very old, because a thick layer of dust made it impossible to see what was inside. I picked one up, wiped it with my coat sleeve and held it up to the light. Inside was a doll. A little doll submerged in oily liquid.

All the jars had dolls inside. Each one was labelled neatly in black ink. I didn't read the labels. I knew what they said. I backed away and headed towards the exit. I tried to find the stone staircase, but every corner of the cellar disappeared into darkness. The only source of light was behind me. So I stumbled around blindly for a long time, at one stage becoming convinced that I would be stuck in that underground labyrinth forever, but just then I came across a staircase—not the one I'd been looking for, but that didn't matter. I ran up the steps and soon reached a room at ground level. To my surprise, however, I was not in Alois Adler's house but the gardener's cottage. The cottage was cold and deserted. All the windows and doors were locked. It would be foolish to imagine the key was somewhere inside. It was completely dark outside. I decided to sit down and rest, and above all to think, to think things through.

Are you listening to me, doctor?

The face of my wife's psychiatrist had sunk into the darkness, I could barely make out his eyes. There was a clatter of dishes downstairs, dinner was being served. The smell of burnt milk made me feel sick. I needed a breath of fresh air right away. I went over to the window. It was locked. I struggled with the net curtain for a bit, and finally I smashed the glass with my elbow. I had to. A damp gust of November night struck my face. I felt dizzy and thought I was going to faint. So I lay down on the gardener's bed, then nestled my head into the pillow, instinctively tucking my left hand underneath it. I felt a hard object. I took it out and brought it close to my face.

I was holding a pocket diary, but it was too dark to read anything. I put it in my coat pocket and crawled out through the broken window into the garden.

My feet shuffling through the leaves as I walked, I found myself on a path leading to the gate. The blind statues stared at me with their mouths open. I followed the broken branches back to the car.

I started the engine and drove off. Before long, I stopped at a roadside bar for a coffee. I'd had nothing to eat or drink since the previous evening. I ordered a croissant and took the small black diary out of my pocket. It was stuffed with extra pages, folded pieces of paper, receipts and planned expenses. The notes were written in 1956 by Ondre Bianco. I even found a letter he'd written but clearly never sent. His signature was there. But...

Do you believe me?

But it wasn't possible. It was impossible.

After leaving the Third Reich, Ondre headed east and south. From Ukraine, via Romania and South Tyrol to Italy. I set off in his footsteps.

The doctor took something out of a drawer and placed it on the desk. To avoid looking at his hands, I stared out of the window. A group of nurses were walking down the driveway between the trees. They must have finished their shift and were going into town. They quickly disappeared from view.

From Tyrol I followed him to Rome. I was hoping to find out where he'd gone. Argentina, Florida, Chile? Wherever he was, I wanted to track him down and ask what my mother was doing there among those pregnant women he'd gathered on the square next to the well. I wanted to drag the words from his throat, even if I had to reach all the way into his guts.

I went to Rome. Bianco's name appeared in the guest-book at the Bishop's Palace. He'd visited the bishop three times in 1945, and the mayor once. He'd requested an audience with the Pope, but he must have been sent away empty-handed, because he'd left then for Bolzano. He travelled to Bolzano as Ondre.

It was sunny when I arrived in Bolzano. I went to the registration bureau, but they told me to go to the registry office. At the registry office, a woman dressed in black advised me to go to the parish records office. I had a hard job getting my bearings in that city. The little streets leading to the monastery on the hill suddenly turned and fell steeply towards the river, or ended abruptly at the back of tenement houses. No one could give me any information. Whichever way I went, I always ended up in the same place: back in front of the registry office. I felt I was so close to discovering the truth, but at the same time something was holding me back. I thought I'd go mad. I circled around that city like a bird in an aviary or a dog on a lead. I circled, and I couldn't find my way. It was extremely hot.

There was a bar across the street. In desperation I decided to have a vodka. I pushed the door open and went inside. The bartender was drying glasses with a white cloth. I sat on a bar stool and ordered a vodka straight. After the second shot I asked about the parish office. As I drank my fourth, I complained about the incompetence of the registrar in black. I'd just finished my fifth when some regular customers came in. They greeted the bartender with a nod and sat down at a table. I ordered a round and went to join them. We drank. I told them where I was from and what I was looking for. They ordered another round.

'Ondre was an honest man, he never deceived anyone,' said the oldest. 'I know about people. I know what I'm talking about,' he said, ordering another round. We drank.

I woke up in the cemetery. The morning dew was evaporating fast in the first rays of the sun and the cemetery looked incredibly beautiful. I had a vague memory of them taking me there to show me someone's grave, to prove something to me. But why that should have interested me I could not remember. I was leaning against a white marble tomb. I could taste the bitterness of the previous night, my head hurt, I felt like death warmed up. I tried to brush the mud off my coat, but I only succeeded in smearing it over a bigger area. I looked around helplessly for something I could use to smarten myself up, but this was a cemetery, not a dry cleaner's. A black placard was hanging from a cross hammered into a mound of earth. With difficulty, I focused on the silver-white lettering. I blinked and looked again. By the cemetery wall was the grave of Ondre Bianco, whose soul was commended to the Lord in March 1946.

I'd been searching for him all these years, and he'd died long ago. I was right on his heels, following his every move, while he was dead and buried. He'd made a mockery of me. I hated him with all my heart, with all my strength.

A bell rang out from a high tower. I fell to my knees. Every chime echoed many times over in my heart. The bell's ringing and my pain rent the morning air. I fell face-down and sank my teeth into the wet earth. I bit, scratched and tore at the earth until I had no strength left and all I could do was lie on his grave, my cheek pressed against the cold, black ground as if it were a pillow. I reached deeper with my left hand. There was no diary. He was dead. I was on his grave. I checked the parish records. He'd died. You understand, doctor? He'd died, he couldn't have written a letter ten years later. He'd died, he couldn't have been keeping his accounts. There was no diary.

One evening, alone at home, I opened a tin of sardines and a bottle of beer. I turned on the TV. One of the news headlines was about the Balkans conflict. Soldiers were guarding some tents. The cloudless Croatian sky above them, white birds flapping their wings. The system had changed, the map of the world had changed. I'd been cut off, discarded. I felt as if I'd wasted my life. I'd been looking for him the whole time, but I'd been too late. I couldn't forgive myself for that. Maybe if I'd tried harder? Maybe if I'd put in more effort?

And then I saw him. He was there. Standing to the side, his face turned towards the sun. I saw his sharp profile, white hair at his temples, bushy eyebrows. He was there. A moment later, the report ended and the camera returned from Srebrenica to the studio.

But I knew his face, I'd have recognised it 100 years from now, even 1,000. Whatever name he was hiding under. I had seen him.

I started searching again.

Do you know what I'm saying?

I decided to trace all the places I knew he'd been, everything I knew about him. To do so, I bought a large map. It was six feet square. I laid it out on the floor, it didn't fit on the table.

I marked his grave in Bolzano with the date of his death in red pen. The documents from Bydgoszcz, including my mother's deportation order from 1939. The photograph from the square with the well in 1940. The gardener's house in black, 1956. Antwerp in the 1970s. The footage from Sarajevo and Srebrenica, 1995.

I didn't give in, I kept searching. Listen to me, doctor.

I read his notes and memos in the black diary. Not everything was legible; some of the entries looked like a list of expenses, but the information was encrypted. I didn't want to believe it. I read them many times, over and over. And then… I discovered he'd been planning a trip to America by sea. Of course! I wanted to check. I had to check. I went there. Introduced myself as a researcher. They showed me to a modern vault in the port archives and left me there alone. I could take photocopies, make comparisons. Everything was arranged by date, partially digitised. First, I searched for Andrija Bianco, then Ondre, but no one by either name had left the port in 1956 or later. I kept looking. I checked the passenger lists of all ships going to America. Month by month, row by row. His notebook lay on the table in front of me. I compared the signatures. It took an awfully long time.

In the evening, the cleaner looked in and told me to come back tomorrow. When I was in the corridor, I remembered I hadn't eaten, drunk or been to the toilet all day. I turned left, headed for the toilet rather than the lift. I locked the cubicle door so I wouldn't be disturbed, and suddenly the light went out. I stood still. I was afraid to piss in case I splashed the floor. It would be easy to miss in the dark. I couldn't leave the cubicle because my trousers were down around my ankles, and anyway, I really needed to piss. So I stood there as long as it took for my eyes to adjust to the darkness so that I could make out the shape of the toilet. Then I urinated and left.

The whole lower-ground floor was in total darkness and there were no light switches anywhere. It ran on photocells, which had just gone off, so there was nothing I could do. The lift wasn't working. I set off down the corridor, which led right, then left, before I came to a door. I pushed the door handle. I was expecting to find a staircase, but I was wrong.

Instead, I found myself in a large room lit faintly by LEDs and sensors. It looked like some kind of boiler room. Half the space was taken up by a huge black stove. It was cold. Its chrome lid was covered with little red flashing lights.

The opposite wall was lined with shelves stacked with papers for burning. Old maps, cross-sections of big sailing boats and tattered documents. There were remarkably few of them. I looked through them all.

Do you believe me, doctor? He was there. Multiple times in 1439 and again in 1492. He had his own ship. His signature was there in ten different rows. He bought and sold, transported and brokered. He paid duties and taxes. He'd been here before, you understand? I found him in 1515 and 1660. His credentials were preserved. In 1880 he was sailing back and forth between Africa and Europe. What was he shipping? I don't know. But his signature was on those documents, I swear to God. It was him. Don't you believe me?

I rolled up one of his maps. I hid it under my shirt and when the cleaner opened up in the morning, I slipped out through a side door. They didn't notice anything was missing. They probably have no idea to this day.

I went home and compared his handwriting from the diary with the writing on the map, where he'd marked his location according to the stars. I have his notebook with me. I always carry it with me. Have a look. It's the same handwriting. Black ink on paper, gold shavings on parchment. The same hand. You see?

Don't you believe me?

Total darkness had fallen in the room, but for some reason the doctor hadn't turned on the lamp. It was pitch-black. The noises of the psychiatric hospital were gradually subsiding.

The wind outside had stripped the trees of their leaves. They stood in a line now, naked, bald, swollen, looking at the black birds circling overhead.

The Station

The snitches have fish lips and small tits.

'Sir,' they say to the ward head, 'he tried to escape again last night,' they say.

'We called security, sir.'

'You should have called me.' The ward head has a moustache, he's hoarse in the morning from lack of sleep. He comes over to the bed, checks the file and the temperature chart. He sits down on the edge of the bed, pulling his trouser legs up only a little so as not to show his hairy calves, and shakes my skinny shoulders. I'm lying with my back to him.

'If you don't want to talk to me, I'll come back in the afternoon,' he says, and prescribes oxycodone injections into my bottom.

'Please let me know when he falls asleep,' he whispers to the nurse and walks away, and I'm left alone. My face towards the wall. My backside in the air for all to see.

Sometimes I get so discouraged that I lie down on the ground like that, and I lie there in that safe position until the end of time. Let them leave me there. Let me lie here, don't pick me up, I whisper into the floorboards, I speak nicely, please leave me alone, miss, please, or I'll smash your head in and everyone will see your brains strewn across the wall. Sometimes this boundlessness comes over me, piss off, you bitch, don't touch me with your dirty fingers that were just moments ago digging around in some palliative care patient's rectum, get the fuck off me. And then suddenly there are four of them and they're tugging me, lifting me, carrying me. *Away from me, all you who do evil, if the Lord is with me, who can be against me?* But I don't have claws, they blunted my claws. I don't have fangs. They removed my fangs. If I could just wring their necks! I toss my helpless head until the blonde Charlie's Angel uncovers my skinny old backside, go on, I say, go on, undress me, you slut, undress me, what you're looking for is lower down, until the blonde Angel jabs me with a megadose, and what would the doctor say, I ask politely, if you kill me, you'll be locked up for life, there's no buffer, no doctor would take responsibility, I say, and I can't hear myself, and I don't believe myself, and I'm suddenly overcome with despair.

And I feel like crying because I don't think I'll ever get out of here. There's no way out of here. There's no way out of here. I'm their hostage. A prisoner. A condemned man. And tears stream down my dry, sunken cheeks and they don't drip on to my pyjama top but soak instead into the crevices and disappear between the cracks in the earth. Then my eyes are red and itchy. *My eyes grow weak with sorrow; they fail because of all my foes.* I wipe them with my hands, permanently cold, bony and trembling.

The truth is, I wouldn't let myself out of here. I wouldn't let myself out.

I tried to leave a few times, just leave, get dressed and leave, there's nothing more natural. You simply get dressed and you leave. What could be simpler? But no, no, no! Don't get any ideas!

The ward head, Uncle Marek, remember Uncle Marek? Your mother's younger brother? We brought him a nylon shirt once, he cried when he saw it… So the ward head, Uncle Marek, remember Uncle Marek? Ah, I already asked, you remember, of course you do, you don't forget stuff like that. So every day he sits on the edge of my hospital bed, unbuttons his lab coat, pulls up his trouser leg, lays his knee on the starched sheet and says you must come by sometime when I'm on the night shift, old boy. That's what your mother's brother says to me; I used to tease him that, despite all his studying, he'd never amount to much, he'd only get some menial job at the hospital stoking the fires. He was already smoking like a chimney back then. He used to take fags out of my pocket, he thought I didn't know, he still denies it now. A nineteen-year-old boy with a mop of blond hair, I remember him as if it were yesterday, in blue Wranglers and a bright shirt, your mother and I brought it back for him from Yugoslavia. He was nineteen years old, did I say that? He comes by every day, he sits down or takes me for a walk in the garden. No one dares disturb us. Ward head of geriatrics. These days, you could pass as a patient on your own ward! That's what I told him. Good one, right?

I'd told him before that I wanted to get out, but he just laughed.

'You don't like it here, old boy, I send you my prettiest nurses and you complain. Don't you like it here? With Charlie's Angels at your bedside?'

'No. I want to get out, I must get out.'

'No chance,' he said, shaking his head.

But today I went to his office and put a letter on his desk.

'What the fuck is that?' He was smoking by the window.

'At my own request, aware…'

'Aware? Bullshit.'

'…aware of the consequences…'

'You have no clue what you're saying.'

'…aware of the consequences of leaving…'

'Cut the crap.'

'…the consequences of leaving the palliative care ward.'

He flicked his cigarette through the open window. 'You won't get far.'

'No need to threaten me. I know what's wrong with me.'

'So what do you think is wrong with you?' he asked, his voice so sweet that I understood in that instant how he managed it with all those women, the motherfucker.

I just shrugged. What's wrong with me? Old age.

'I give you twelve hours.'

I stood there in silence. What did that mean, he'd give me something? I don't want anything from you, you little shit. That's what I told him. He laughed in my face. You've got twelve hours. He wrote me out a pass. Pressed it into my hand and pushed me out of the door.

I stood in the corridor in my pyjamas and felt slippers, which I hated with all my heart.

There was a train to where you live at 6.47 p.m. It was five o'clock. I had to take a shower, shave, get dressed. Fetch my overcoat and shoes from the cloakroom. My wallet and the medallion were in the safe.

I decided to call you from the station.

We'll arrive on schedule at 6.15 a.m., said the conductor, and I believed him.

I found a seat in a non-smoking compartment by the window. I took off my overcoat and hung it on a hook branded with the State Railways logo. Seven minutes until departure. Seven minutes. I called you from the station.

The kettle's whistling. I come out of the bathroom wrapped in a towel. I leave wet footprints on the floor. Pour myself a cup of coffee and go back to the bathroom.

I'm really longing to see you, Dad.

'I'm arriving on the train tomorrow at 6.15 a.m.' I heard your voice on the other end of the phone and suddenly I was out of breath, like the time in PE when something happened and at first everyone ran away in a panic, then the next moment all the adults, the teacher, the head and the caretaker, were standing over me, watching to see if I'd survive. I get it from Mum. I'm a survivor.

After all those years without seeing each other, I couldn't leave you waiting. Six fifteen in the morning. It's still dark at that time in December.

'I want to talk to you.'

You want to talk to me. That's what you said. That's what you said on the phone. Finally, after so many years, six o'clock at the station.

Straight away, I was longing to see you.

I had no luggage with me. I made a call from a payphone at the station. Just one call. I'm coming, I'll be at the station at 6.15 a.m. and I want to talk to you.

I had no luggage with me. I put my wallet in my coat pocket.

I had no luggage with me, but I bought a newspaper from a station kiosk. I'd no intention of reading it. I hadn't the slightest interest in current affairs, but I feared intrusive travel companions. I needed something to separate myself from them. The *Życie* daily worked perfectly. Perfectly.

It wasn't that easy, you know. You were searching for something your whole life.

When I was still at school, you used to take me to the archives in Bydgoszcz. After the war, the documents needed to be put in order. It's damned important, you said, to determine the shape of the façade, define the architectural elements and restore the body of the building, you said. That's what you said, and you told me to look for photographs, sketches, drawings, plans, maps, testaments. Anything that could help you with the reconstruction. You were looking too. What were you looking for then?

'Open up the cellars,' you told the officials, and a young woman in a grey dress started to gasp like a mouse dying of a heart attack.

I actually do know what a mouse dying of a heart attack sounds like, if you can believe it.

'No one's been down there since the war.'

'Then it's about time.' You fix her with an icy glare.

The view through the window. Cold outside. The ground frozen over, the air still. Some part of me suddenly saw a dark army. Black boots, steady stride. Captain Degrelle takes the salute. No, it's not possible. It must be a memory from a photograph, there were so many of them that day.

'But that's where the Germans imprisoned all the women who worked at the office, since then…'

You didn't allow her to finish her sentence. You let her go first. We went down the steps.

'It wasn't the Germans. It was a unit from northern Flanders in Belgium.'

So it was Degrelle after all.

The faint light in the cellars. The cold and damp. You told me to look through the records, you were searching for something behind the cabinets. My fingers went numb from the cold. I remember the smell of the damp, musty files. The smell of mould. The woman stood in the doorway, freezing, rubbing her arms. It looked as if she were hugging herself. Your gaze fell on her like a hawk's. Did you meet up with her at the hotel?

'I'm cold.' My voice sounded metallic, my whole body ached.

'We're done for today. Note down which name you're on.'

Mum was no longer with us then.

I took a seat in a non-smoking compartment by the window. I hung my overcoat on the hook and put my newspaper on the fold-down table branded with the State Railways logo. I crossed my legs. Waited for my travel companions. I was curious about them, genuinely.

The train was standing at platform two, the departure time came and went. We were delayed by three minutes. Finally, there was a sharp jerk and my journey began.

A moment later, a man and a woman came into the compartment, I guessed they were a married couple, he was wearing a jacket, she a brown skirt, no doubt some kind of office worker. They sat by the door. She took out a book. I tried to make out the title but, not wanting to be intrusive, I had to abandon my attempts. I tried not to impose my presence on them, I said nothing and looked out of the window.

We passed the last buildings on the outskirts of the city. Before us, a space was opening up that I remembered well from my childhood.

My father.

My father, your grandfather, travelled to work every day by train. His overcoat hung in the hallway and smelled of something distant and unattainable. Your grandfather, remember, was a teacher of geography and cartography before the war. And he was very successful in his field. Were it not for the outbreak of war, he would certainly have become the headteacher of the secondary school in Bydgoszcz. He was a strict and exacting teacher.

Mother.

She worked in an office in Bydgoszcz. She used to kneel down in front of me to tie my shoelaces.

'Sorry, I need some fresh air,' I say to them, and squeeze between their knees. The man in the jacket reluctantly makes room for me.

'Of course.'

His woman presses her knees against the edge of the red State Railways seat. As I pass, I brush against her skirt.

Out in the corridor, I open the window and a rush of air hits me in the face. The first breath. Painful freedom. I watched his death without remorse. I hid behind the onlookers' backs, I saw everything. A round of gunfire, and silence. Their bodies were left by the church wall. I'd spoken to him the day before. I wanted to ask him something. 'Dad, can I ask you something?' 'Of course.'

'Can I ask you something?' The man in the jacket is standing next to me.

'Of course.'

He takes out his cigarettes, offers me one, I take it.

'Are you feeling all right?'

Am I feeling all right?

I really was longing to see you. I didn't want you to be waiting for me at the station. But of course, things don't always go according to plan for me. Minor delays mean that suddenly I'm not where I should be.

When did we last see each other?

You came out to meet us in the courtyard. You were wearing a bottle-green corduroy jacket. It was always hanging in the hallway. I remember how it held the scent of your aftershave and cigarettes. And the smell of the

Zaporozhets, with the faulty heating that had to be on all year round.

So you came to us in the courtyard, and we were standing there smoking cigarettes, strong, unfiltered. Today, one of those would kill me for sure. So we stood in front of you and waited for you to do something or say something. You came to us in just a jacket. Bottle-green against concrete-grey. Your hands weren't shaking, your brow didn't even twitch. You informed us that the police were asking for our names. They needed forty names on the list. 'You'd better be creative,' you said. 'And careful,' you added, 'that no random people end up there.' Random people. Who started laughing first? Me. I've always known when you were joking. I know what to expect from you. Who was forty-first on the list? Me. I know your jokes. I know what to expect from you.

When they came for me in the morning, the wheezing started. I was out of breath again. You opened the door for them. There were no allowances in your world. Even for me. Especially for me.

I was really longing to see you. But the preparations for leaving the house took longer than usual.

A grey cardigan. Buttons. The dust you brushed off as if our life depended on it. It did. Now I know that it did. When that man was leading me away, his black hair combed back and shining with pomade, you silently, silently brushed some dust from my jumper as if it meant something.

They led me out at dawn. A light bulb right in my eyes.

The conductor came at night. Tickets, please. Here. Fuck off, shithead. Thank you. Don't thank me, you son of a bitch.

My documents were in order, but the man in the jacket and his travel companion were in the wrong seats. They tried to explain, they made excuses, they pleaded. It didn't work. He led them out of the compartment. We didn't even say goodbye.

After their abrupt departure, I felt unexpectedly lonely. As if I were alone in the world, travelling with no purpose or plan. Night had fallen, thick, outside the window.

They took my father at night too. Shot him the next day.

My mother didn't come home from work. She didn't come home in the evening. She didn't come home at night. She didn't come home in the morning. She didn't come home all the days after that. I didn't keep count, there were so many. I had to go on living.

I must have dozed off, because I was awoken by a light bulb shining right in my eyes. The light had been turned on in the compartment. My senile face was reflected in the glass. To avoid looking at it, I tried to read. It was a tedious activity and I struggled to make sense of it.

After midnight, someone yanked the door open and a woman entered the compartment. She had a red leather suitcase and handbag and was dressed in leather from head to toe.

'Is the seat next to you free?'

All the seats around me were free.

'Could I ask for your help? It's not heavy.'

I could barely lift her luggage. My muscles aren't what they used to be.

'May I ask where you're going? And you haven't spoken a word to your son in forty years? Never, not even at Christmas? You must have been very lonely.'

I must.

I met your mother when I was twenty years old. We were working together on the Party committee. I was in the field, she was in the office. Yes. I was very lonely then.

You had to, I know you had to. But…

I know, and as for me… But…

When I got home, a faint smell of you was lingering on the coat stand in the hallway. The cigarette had stopped smouldering in the ashtray a long time ago. The mark left by the shaving brush on the bathroom shelf and the empty hook where a dressing gown used to hang. You left a few bits and pieces you didn't need any more. A pencil. A couple of shirts. The cover of your notebook. I know you had to. I know. But…

I always put my glasses in the case. Yes, the one you used when we went on our research trips. Every day, for as long as I've known that my eyesight is deteriorating, every day I reach into that case for my glasses. But today, as I was leaving at 5.52 a.m. to come and meet you at the station, the case was empty. I don't know where… I always put them on the windowsill. My glasses. I can't come and meet you at the station without my glasses. Five fifty-seven in the morning. They were in the bedroom, I'd used them as a bookmark. I have this dreadful habit of leaving teaspoons, pencils and pens to mark my place in books, papers, piles of documents. Sorry. I've done it again.

You only took me with you on Saturdays after school. For an inventory of former German buildings, on a research trip to the archives, or to pick up some records. You showed me how to read realities from fragments of old photographs, images, inaccurate maps, land records and private wills. You showed me all kinds of maps.

On Sundays, we went to visit Mum.

The train travelled into the night. The lights of unfamiliar cities flashed past beyond the window. We passed through station after station so quickly I didn't have time to read their names.

The woman in leather talked an awful lot. It exhausted me so much that I had to leave several times under the pretext of using the bathroom. In the end, I shielded myself from her with my copy of *Życie*. I didn't even try to concentrate on the text—in the light of the flickering fluorescent lamp that would have been torture for my eyes. Eventually she fell asleep, lulled by my silence and the steady clattering of the wheels. It must have been around two in the morning. Her head was leaning back against the headrest. This meant I could have a good look at her, undisturbed.

At first, when she entered the compartment, I had thought her quite attractive. But now, looking at her, I found her repulsive. She had varicose veins on her hands and an enlarged, pulsing artery on her neck. Every ten seconds or so she gulped, her throat moving as if something were alive inside it. Disgusting. Sweaty forehead, messy hair. Face powder dampened with skin secretions, mascara, eye shadow. Lipstick-stained teeth showed between her parted lips. I couldn't take my eyes off them. There was something so vulgar about those smudged lips, something so obscene, that I moved closer. So close, I could smell her stale breath. And then she suddenly opened her eyes and saw me, my face right above hers. I was scared she'd scream, but she started laughing. Hysterical and loud. It was how your mother used to laugh when we were eating and before we… She would laugh so unreservedly, absolutely, completely. Desperately, insanely, hopelessly. She would laugh until she ran out of breath, until she collapsed. Her face twisted, her body shook with spasms and she went rigid. We called doctors, psychiatrists, the emergency services, and in the end Uncle Marek put her in an institution.

And this woman was the same. She started to laugh the same way. I couldn't shut her up. I put my hand over her mouth, but she bit me and grew even more furious, overwhelmed by a mixture of sobbing and… I squeezed with both hands, clamped them over her mouth and nostrils. I had to.

I had to. I looked at her tilted head, her closed eyes. Took her ticket from her handbag and laid it on the table beside her. I got up and went in search of another compartment.

We visited your mother at the facility every Sunday. There was no public announcement for her funeral. It was just me, Uncle Marek and the priest. I don't remember if it was early spring or late autumn, but there were no leaves on the trees and I was terribly cold in just my black overcoat. What year was that?

After so many years of silence, I couldn't leave you waiting at the station. My watch. I had to get the watchmaker to change my strap recently. The old one was worn through and almost... But the new one is so stiff, it's hard to fasten it on my left wrist.

'You could wear your watch on your right hand,' you said. You had a point, but it's habit, you know. So I fasten the strap, I don't know which hole. Yes, it's your watch. You left it in your desk drawer. It was overwound. Took a day to repair. It runs exactly on time. The hands are pointing to five past six. I need ten minutes to get to the station. I can't leave you waiting. Wallet in my coat pocket, I hope it's not snowing. Keys. The keys were in the door. They were in the lock outside all night. I don't remember. I forget so many things, I'm sorry.

Time matters, you said.

Was it possible not to believe you? I remember your pocket diaries, with writing all over, even in the margins, scraps of paper stuck in, notes on the covers. 'This is my portable memory,' you said, blowing cigarette smoke right in my face. It stung my eyes, but I didn't mind.

'I need to talk to you,' you said on the phone. You need to talk to me. You called after all these years. You remembered the phone number, you called. You're alive.

I was forgotten as though I were dead, abandoned outside the walls of Hebron like a dog, I am just a big nobody. But I await your words like a reprieve, like a scrap of meat thrown to the dogs.

I moved to another compartment, the other passengers looked at me with indifference.

'Are you going far?'

'All the way.'

'And where from, if you don't mind my asking?'

'From the north, my father came from the north. I'm a descendent of the great Stübben, Hermann Joseph Stübben, have you heard of him? Oh! A fine pre-war urban planner, city planner, a visionary, an architectural genius. Aachen, Luxembourg, Cologne. Poznań! Bydgoszcz. His plans of Bydgoszcz were unparalleled, unparalleled. I'm a city planner too, in a way. My modest contribution can also be admired.' I cleared my throat. The passengers fell silent.

My career. My mouth filled with bitter saliva. I felt the urge to spit it out. I went into the corridor and opened a window. It was getting light in the east. I stared out into the gloom. The train seemed to be going in the wrong direction. Never mind.

Then… no! Sorry, it was earlier, it must have been earlier, when I appeared before you on behalf of the Party. You stood in neat, concentric semicircles, each of you with a cigarette pressed between your lips. And you.

I had to, I simply had to.

Anyway, it was all after that, everything just got screwed up. You understand? It wasn't worth a thing. It wasn't worth a thing. Not a thing.

My glasses are fogging up, my mind too. *The padding of my words. A rag of language. I used it to wipe foreign soil, my tongue licked their feet. I used up all my saliva in the service of a false god, waited in vain for my reward.*

The train seemed to be going in the opposite direction. A sleepy railway worker in a white coat walked past me. Hey! Don't I know you from somewhere? He shrugged.

I stepped inside the first empty compartment.

It's colder outside at night than I thought. A thicker coat would probably have been better.

Precious minutes, and I'm really longing to see you. Keys in the door. Where the hell are my gloves? Six fifteen in the morning.

Uncle Marek called. He asked if you were here. You're not here yet.

Will I even recognise you? What do you look like now?

I'm an old man. I break off speaking in mid-sentence, I don't know where I've stopped, where to begin. It's helpless, involuntary. My head falls on to my chest.

I must have drifted off. I woke up just before six o'clock. We were nearing the end of the line.

And then I realised that it wasn't my fault. That I am merely *a lute in the Lord's hand, his weapon.* That it never ends. That they will always be this way. That they are. That we are.

Sometimes we worked through the night. Let him lie in his own blood, leave him, I said. In the morning I looked the boys in the eye. Leave him there! And I walked away. They stayed behind. After nights like that I couldn't sleep. My whole body ached. It's hard to describe what it's like when your whole body aches. I lay down on my bunk and tried to sleep. But I couldn't. I thought about those who had stayed behind. Now I don't feel such pity. I even think... I know it's terrible, but I even think maybe it's better that way. It's possible to believe that they weren't... That they aren't people.

It's easy to believe that.

God, it's so easy to believe. To do and to believe.

God, my God, take my mind, take my memory. Take it, You can fucking have it, I am but a lute in the hand of the Lord, how easy it is to be good in His name, His anger is just and right, it falls upon all my enemies. Take Your goodness and fuck off. For my immoral deeds have outgrown me, they weigh too heavily on me like an excess burden.

I quit after one of them died of a heart attack.

'You've got twelve hours. I give you twelve hours.' That's what he told me. Who told me that?

The train pulled into the station with a long hiss. The conductor helped me step down on to the platform. *Away from me, evil-doer, get back, enemy,* I said to him boldly.

'No luggage, sir?'

I shook my head. Through the window, I saw my overcoat hanging next to the woman in leather. I decided not to go back for it. I straightened up and walked off down the street.

Did we arrange to meet at the station or at home?

I'm late, but I hope you'll wait. I'm just longing to see you, Dad. So I'm walking down Station Road, which leads in one direction towards the station, in the other towards the cemetery—but who'd want to live on Cemetery Road? I pass tenement blocks, passageways and underpasses. I know all the homeless people here, the hoodlums, prostitutes and degenerates. I've always known them. And then I see someone sitting in a doorway without an overcoat.

'Is everything OK?' I ask, hoping that it is, and that I'll make it in time to meet you at the station. But he shakes his head and I can see the despair in his eyes.

'What's your name? Where do you live?'

'I can't remember.'

You understand? He can't remember. At half past six in the morning, he can't remember.

I know you'll leave in a minute and we'll never see each other again. But...

I really am longing... You got in touch with me. You called. But...

So he could be your age. A buttoned-up grey woollen cardigan from which someone probably used to brush invisible specks of dust as if it mattered. A medallion hangs from his neck, he's turning it awkwardly between his fingers.

'Show me that.'

Handmade by one of the Italian masters. You taught me to recognise good craftsmanship. The saint's profile was depicted with sharp, mean features. Like my grandfather's features. Like your features. Like mine.

'Show me that.'

I try to take the chain off his neck, but the old man's strong hand tightens in an iron-like grip around my left wrist. The pain pierces me to the core.

No, surely he's older. He must be over eighty; his grip reminds me of something. Those are the hands of the man who stood in the dark behind the light bulb. The one who stared at me when I was haunted by the kind of nightmares that only come at night. After that, reality seemed the best of all possible worlds.

I focus on the medallion.

'*Cosmographus incomparabilis.* The unparalleled cartographer,' I read.

You put a lot of effort into my Latin. But when asked what you were looking for, you laughed hoarsely, drew on your cigarette and said you'd know when you found it. Or another time, that you were looking for city maps from before the Second World War to help you reconstruct the towers of the Jesuit church, which was demolished in the autumn of 1939 when the Germans—not the Germans—when the Waffen-SS, that's better, on a Sunday morning, they shot some people against the walls of the Jesuit church, whom did they shoot against the walls of the Jesuit church, Dad? When they shot my father, when they shot, and I stood and watched, because one group of people was shooting another and it didn't matter who was shooting whom, because it's only ever people shooting people. *They had faith in You, our fathers, they trusted, but You did not rescue them; they cried out to You and were not saved, they believed You and they were let down.* And that's why you're looking for Hermann Stübben's plans? Yes.

I touch the medallion hanging from his neck. Then he crushes my wrist with his iron-like grip.

The morose profile of that damned saint. Fra Mauro, I say, and the man looks up. Beneath his white eyebrows, his eagle-like eyes shine, though the irises have grown watery over time, but the pupils, his pupils, black and deep, penetrate the soul. I try in vain to break free of his grasp. I only manage to free the cuff of my coat. The watch is pinned to my veins. In the light of the street lamp, 6.37 a.m. You're not waiting for me at the station.

Snow begins to fall on the street. The city is enveloped in total silence.

He's sitting on the steps of an abandoned tenement house on Station Road, his white head leaning against the wall. He must have had raven-black hair, I think, imagining the man thirty, forty years younger, as I'm being led away at night and you're brushing dust from the grey cardigan, and later, when he stands behind me with his hair combed high, shining like a bird's feather on his temples, and I know he's about to ask the question.

What were we fighting for? For freedom of what? Speech?

And now I'm kneeling in front of him with my wrist trapped in the shackles of his grip, my face so close to his face that I can hear his breathing fading, I can hear his thoughts. In the quiet of the night I breathe his breath, I think his words. You understand?

The express train to Warsaw leaves in six minutes, and from there… We'll never see each other again. Dad.

'Who are you?'

'I can't remember.'